SANS MOI

SANS MOI

MARIE DESPLECHIN

Translated from the French

by Will Hobson

THOMAS DUNNE BOOKS
ST. MARTIN'S PRESS
NEW YORK

FIRST PART

I

'Thanks, I'd love some more,' said Olivia, taking the handle of the saucepan. 'I've got a confession to make. God, I should stop eating so much, I'm blowing up like a balloon . . . Do you remember when I first came here, in September?'

'Yes,' I said. 'It's still only October, after all.'

'Oh. Right. Well, I've got to tell you this. I hadn't stopped taking drugs back then. I admit it.'

'Uh huh.' I reached for my cigarettes.

'But I have now.'

I lit a cigarette unhurriedly, blew a smoke ring, and said, 'I knew.'

'You knew what?'

'I knew you were taking drugs.'

Olivia wiped her plate with a piece of bread in silence. She didn't look up. Maybe she didn't believe me, or perhaps she was hurt.

'You could have just kicked me out. People don't like babysitters using drugs.'

'If it'd been anyone else, I would have.' I didn't say anything else.

She got up from the table and cleared away our plates, piling them noisily on top of each other.

'Do you want some coffee?' she asked, going into the kitchen.

I could hear her in there, muttering about the little espresso maker. I'd screwed the top on too tightly and she couldn't open it.

'The fact is,' I shouted, 'I didn't sack you because I trust you . . . Can you hear me? Because I'm fond of you.'

A furious groan came from the kitchen, followed by a familiar crash.

'Don't worry,' Olivia called out. 'It's not serious, it's only the glasses.'

As a rule, we appreciate the love of our fellow human beings either as a necessary acknowledgement of our worth or as a surprise that seems heaven sent. We have been raised for it, one way or another – by being starved or over-indulged, it doesn't really matter. When it comes down to it, we love to be loved and we love to love, maybe misguidedly and to our cost, but deliberately, stubbornly and repetitively. Love pleases us, with its rattle of chains and periodic windfalls. Good thing too. There's nothing more desolate than hating love.

Olivia was caving in under the weight of her problems. Having experienced neither starvation nor over-indulgence, only absence and chaos, she was as mistrustful of other people's feelings as a petty criminal.

'Did someone say something to you?' she asked, slapping two sugars down on the table next to my cup.

'No,' I said. 'I guessed. It wasn't that hard.'

In order to confirm my suspicions, one morning I'd summoned to my flat my brother Laurent, a family counsellor, and his friend Thierry, an expert in the field, partly reformed but full of regrets and prone to relapses.

'Tell him what you told me on the phone,' my brother said, sitting on the old Fender amplifier which presided over the trestle table in my flat.

I poured a cup of coffee.

'OK. Well, some evenings she doesn't say a word and she's really down, and then the next day she's all excited and bright-eyed and can't stop talking.'

'Yes,' said the expert.

'She talks the whole time about the pills she's taking or that she used to take and about drinking, but she swears: drugs, no way, what a bloody liability, when you see how it messes people up, especially girls, all the things you can't do when you're into it and how they all end up, no teeth and on the game, and so on and so forth. Unless you're in it up to your eyeballs, I don't see how anybody could go on about it so much.'

'Sure,' the expert said, looking concerned. He wasn't much of a talker.

'Guys are always ringing up and she doesn't want to talk to them, it's as if she's scared. Then there's Captain Hook and Long John Silver, in and out of her room at all hours of the day and night, carrying bags and acting like big shots – the concierge is going crazy with suspicion. Then there's the packages she has to deliver, by taxi – who to and with what money, I've no idea. One evening she told me that she'd taken my daughter with her to drop something off. A trip in a taxi, that's fun for a kid. I said no, there's nothing fun about it and that from now on there is going to be no more talk of packages or taxis.'

'Well done. Any other signs?'

'The tin foil keeps going missing from the kitchen.'

'Oh no!' said the expert. 'Tin foil's a problem. A big problem.'

He hunched over his coffee.

'You see?' said Laurent.

'No chance this'll sort itself out,' the expert diagnosed, scratching his sparse hair in dismay. 'Every chance it'll get worse.'

'You're fucked,' concluded Laurent. 'She's got to go. We can tell her, if you like.'

'No,' I said, 'let me sort this out. It's a special case.'

At that point, my brother left for work and the dismayed expert stayed behind with me. We went to bed straight away since it was only casual between us – to my great displeasure. I would have preferred a little regularity.

'The hardest thing,' I told Olivia, so she'd understand all the anxiety she'd caused me, 'was that I didn't want you to leave.'

'Because of the children?'

'Yes. But because of me as well. I didn't want to sack you, I didn't want to give you a hard time. I just wanted you to stop taking drugs.'

Of the prize-winning line-up of liars and addicts life had thrown up for me to become attached to, it was clear that she took the palm, the laurel wreath, the roar of the crowd and the entire triumphal arch. It was also clear, from the day we met, that I felt as if I'd known her for ever. Don't get me wrong. I'm not saying I felt I knew what kind of life she'd had but she struck me as someone I'd always known – the features of her face, the way she laughed and suddenly turned sad. I could tell her socks in the washing machine by their colours. I could recognize her creases in the ironing.

Let's say we'd experienced the same fears and hardships and had the same kind of childhood. Or let's say that we were the same age. Smoked the same cigarettes. Wore the same nail varnish. But none of this was the case. I was ten years older than her and our lives were as foreign to one another as a Joanna Trollope novel is to a Hubert Selby short story.

'What about your friends, Agnès and all that lot who sent me to you? Did you ask them?'

'Of course. They all swore no, no drugs, ever. They thought it was amazing, really, considering what you'd been through: no drugs and no prostitution – for a girl who's been in care and lived on the street and seen what she's seen, it's practically a miracle; you can take her on with complete confidence. What's more, she loves children.'

Olivia giggled. She adored people she could make fools of.

'You can't hold it against them. They didn't know. Jean-Luc, Dominique and Agnès, they're innocent. I wouldn't ever have wanted them to suspect.'

'You remind me of a girl I used to know ten years ago. A girl from Savoy. She had tiny blue eyes, thin lips and shoulders like a wrestler. I got her a job at my work. "I wouldn't say I've never touched drugs," she used to say to me, "but all that's over now, it was too much." At lunch she'd tell me about all the tragic things she'd been through, her father who worked in a slate quarry, her twelve brothers and sisters and what a cruel place the world was. The next morning she'd come to the office still a complete mess from the night before, with her clothes all crumpled and white specks round her nostrils and fall asleep on the switchboard. She went mad when someone suggested she should clean up and go into detox and then one morning she left with the four thousand francs I'd lent her; I was earning seven at the time. It made me sad that she could just disappear like that, even though we were friends. I've never seen her again. Maybe she's dead.'

'Maybe,' said Olivia. 'Addicts always end up being bastards, that's just the way they are.'

2

'We should buy a TV for your room,' I said, the day after her confession. 'We can go to Darty while the children are at their father's.'

'Alright,' Olivia said. 'It'll help me sleep. I can't sleep at night. I just feel too awful when I'm on my own.'

'It's because you're up in the maid's room; it's too small.'

'No, I don't think so,' Olivia said, 'I like the room, I've never had a place of my own before, with a key and everything. No, it's just that nights are a problem for me. I feel bad during the day, but at night I feel even worse. I have to keep the lights on and the radio turned up.'

'How do you manage?'

We were on the Metro, sitting on the fold-down seats.

'I just do. I hardly ever go out, that way I can be sure I'm not going to meet anyone. Except when I go to Sainte-Anne, to see the psychiatrist who gives me pills. Are you sure you want to buy a TV? It's not worth it if it's just for me.'

In the shop, she maintained a steadfast silence, staring shamefacedly at the floor. The security guard stuck to us like a leech. I bought a blow heater and a little TV which cost just under 2,000 francs. We got a taxi home, took the lift to the sixth floor and then the back stairs to the seventh. Olivia didn't say a word and I carried the TV the whole way. It was disconcerting leaving it all in her room — the TV, the heater and Olivia.

I went back down to my flat slightly crestfallen. I wasn't used to people not saying thank you. So I told myself she was probably thanking me that very minute, in her heart of hearts, or that she would later, when she'd taken stock, or that I was just mad to want everyone to thank me wholeheartedly all the time for my patience and my goodness.

The children weren't at home so I switched on the Mac and started work. I was feeling facetious. 'Faced with a market which every year becomes marginally more cut-throat due to the extortion rackets run by monopolies, the slaves and their overseers have adapted their exploitative practices in an unending pursuit of greater synergy, productivity and quality,' I typed. Then I reread what I'd written and changed 'cut-throat' to 'demanding', 'the extortion rackets run by monopolies' to 'the effects of globalization', 'the slaves and their overseers' to 'the group's male and female employees' and 'exploitative' to 'working'. I worked as a freelance for several PR companies.

When I was in a good mood, I'd compare my professional activities to those of an embalmer. I'd be given a pile of decomposing lies which had to be made presentable by means of a laborious patchwork of generalities, untruths and utterly meaningless phrases. The great skill lay in preserving an appearance of reality while gutting the document of its contents and stuffing it with hay. A process which simultaneously demanded the technique of a butcher and the light touch of a make-up artist. Through practice, I'd achieved a form of excellence. Of sincerity. Of vulgar, insidious elegance. The PR agencies liked selling me to companies. 'I've brought my pen,' the boss would proclaim to the

client as he walked into his office. With an expansive wave of his arm
he would then reveal me, standing half hidden behind him. 'Yeah,
sure. Pen in the arse,' I'd think, smiling demurely, my briefcase under my
arm. I can't think of any stage in the production of commercial literature which isn't, at heart, stamped with greed and contempt.

That's what I'd think when I was in a good mood.

When I was in a bad mood, I'd drink beer and snivel. Either way, it
amounted to the same thing. The cheques arrived, eventually, and I
paid them into my account.

The ash from my cigarette fell onto the keyboard. I blew it off and
worked on into the evening.

By half-past eight I had finished a thick web of inanities worth
2,000 francs. It was dark and raining. I knew that by this time everyone else would be getting ready to go out without me, and that no
normal person was about to ask me out to dinner, so I poured myself
a glass of red wine and drank it at my table, eyeing the computer
screen. I thought vaguely of the abnormal people likely to show up
on a Saturday evening after half-past eight. Then I tried to calculate
the weight of the hours a person spends alone waiting for sleep to
come on a Saturday night in Paris. Slumped on the sofa, I'd almost
resigned myself to carrying on drinking, when the corridor light
went on.

Olivia came in, blinking.

'Are you still working? I'm going to turn on the light, you can't see
a thing in here.'

A flood of white halogen light suddenly stripped us of shadow and
depth, flattening us like two identical, undercooked crêpes.

Olivia was very pale and had terrible rings round her eyes. But she
was here, she was a living human being, and I was so happy to see her
that I leapt to my feet.

'I didn't know you were still in Paris! I thought you said you were going to see your sister.'

'It seemed better not to,' she said.

'So will you stay and have supper with me?'

'If you like, yes.'

She sat down at the little kitchen table and quietly smoked a cigarette while I cut anything I came across into a thousand little pieces — an onion, a tomato and some very white potatoes which tasted like fruit. The oil sizzled happily in the frying pan, the black rain could fall as much as it wanted, it was winter and we were snug and warm. I picked up the conversation where it had broken off, a few hours earlier.

'Sainte-Anne, why do you go to Sainte-Anne? It's a long way away.'

'I know them.'

'Where from?'

'From before. When I was on the street. One time when I'd had enough of it all and I just wanted a rest, a guy said to me, "All you've got to do is stop eating. You'll pass out and then they have to pick you up." So I stopped eating, passed out, and was picked up by an ambulance. I must have been too young for them to stick me in a hostel or something like that. So I ended up in Sainte-Anne. And, bingo, they looked after me, because I made the nurses and doctors laugh with my stories. After a week, they couldn't keep me in any longer, it's the law, so they called my sister. She didn't want anything to do with me. So the social services came and fetched me. I got shouted at by a judge and then I was back on the outside. "Don't forget to come and see us," the doctor said when I left.

'Later I did go back to see them. They said, "You're a bloody laugh a minute, aren't you? But when you're tired of mucking about and want to get out of this mess, we'll help." And it's true, they seemed pleased when I told them I was giving up. I don't normally tell people I've been in Sainte-Anne's. It makes a bad impression. My sister in particular doesn't want to hear about it. She says all these stories make our family look like trash, first my mother being committed, and then me.'

'Wasn't she an alcoholic, your mother?'

'Yes, but that's not the point. It doesn't matter why you're committed. Committed for this, committed for that, people don't care what for. They'd prefer you weren't committed at all.'

I moved the Macintosh onto the desk in my bedroom while Olivia laid the trestle table. I turned down the light, put on some music and we had supper and chatted.

Here was another reason I hadn't wanted to end our relationship while she was coming off drugs. These chats; I loved just being with her, listening and talking to her. I should add that there were two children who would never have forgiven me if she'd left. She had waited for them outside school every day that autumn, never a minute late, bringing croissants, satchels and manifest friendship, and playing with them for hours on end. I'd hear them laughing from one end of the flat to the other.

When it was time to go to bed, Olivia became vague again.

'Do you mind if I sleep down here?'

'No,' I said. 'I'm afraid of the dark too.'

We laid a mattress out on the living-room floor, and she piled it with blankets. 'Goodnight,' she said. 'Night night,' I answered, 'sleep well,' and I went into my room. I swept away the pile of newspapers that were cluttering up my bed but before lying down, I tiptoed back into the living room.

She was already in a deep sleep, so I switched off the light and the radio.

'Lord, since all of You is contained in even the smallest fragment of Your Creation, You must be somewhere in my crappy life as well.

Besides, I think I can hear You snoring. If You could wake up and give me a little hand, that would be good. You've done it for other people, so why not me? Look after my children with all your might, look after Olivia and look after me, who hasn't got a clue how to come up with twenty thousand francs next month.'

I rolled into a ball, my knees tucked into my stomach. A warm, thick darkness gently rose up inside me. It was sleep coming and I said to myself that this was how I'd like death to be, just like this: gradual, dark and caressing.

3

Drugs, drugs: people get all worked up and no one gets anywhere. It would have been a good thing, at the start, if Olivia had spared me from having to apply a definitive image or name to her condition. We could have told each other stories about our lives without that always taking precedence. With drugs out of the picture, the pain would still be there. But not being invited to consider the one, I could only see the other. At least I wasn't likely to get the issues mixed up.

By the end of October, Olivia had put on ten kilos and was biting her nails to the quick. She temporarily stopped telling me about the ravages of drugs when we were in the kitchen at the start of the evening. To all intents and purposes, she had also stopped talking. Or leaving the building. Or washing her hair. It was only too obvious that this girl wasn't using drugs any more. I put away my suspicions. My anxieties took a new tack.

One evening when I phoned her in her room, I didn't recognize her voice, it was so deep and slow. It shook at every word. I was still afraid that something bad might happen. What the hell could she be doing, all on her own up there in her shoebox, other than dying slowly?

'Can you come down? I need to see you.'

'Right now?' groaned the voice, echoing as if from the bottom of a well. 'Tomorrow morning would be better, I don't feel well.'

'Now, this very minute. If you're not here in five minutes, I'm coming up.'

'No, no,' she answered hurriedly. 'No, wait, I'm coming down, you've woken me up.'

I stuck Thomas and Suzanne in the bath, the taps on full, and dashed into the kitchen, where she was waiting for me, her hair in her face, her eyes vacant and a pair of huge pink velvet slippers on her feet.

'Olivia, stay and have supper with us.'

'I'm not hungry.'

'I don't care. Everyone eats at this hour. Sit down.'

She sat on a chair while I put a pan of water on the stove. I uncorked a bottle and poured two large glasses; not everyone can do without alcohol, at any rate she and I couldn't, particularly at the end of the day.

She took her glass and her eyes filled with tears. I regret writing it so baldly, but there we are, she cried.

Minutes passed. They were very charged minutes, very beautiful and very laboured, which fell between us and set like concrete.

So there we were. Olivia was crying, I was washing the salad and the children were splashing about, sending sheets of water crashing over the edge of the bath like a waterfall. All in all, it was a very homely atmosphere. Then the noodles were cooked, our glasses were empty and it was time to take the pans off the stove and the children out of the water.

'Shall I get them?'

'If you like. I'll lay the table.'

The slippers left the kitchen.

'Olivia, Olivia!' cried Thomas and Suzanne.

'Basically,' said Olivia, 'I don't feel comfortable with people. It's not that I get bored, well yes I do, but there's more to it than that. I feel unhappy. If I had a choice, I'd spend all my time with children.'

Once I'd felt a twinge of conscience about Olivia being shut away for hours with Thomas and Suzanne, tirelessly playing their favourite game over and over and only coming out of their room to stock up on orange juice. So I'd gone down the passage, gently pushed open the bedroom door and watched them, sprawled on the fitted carpet with their little piles of counters in front of them.

Olivia was slapping the floor with the flat of her hand.

'Oh no,' she was saying, 'that's enough Suzanne, you never stop cheating. If you carry on, I'm not going to go on playing, it's too annoying.'

Suzanne took her counters back with a sly expression and threw the dice again.

'She's right,' said Thomas. 'If you carry on we're not going to play with you any more. Your go, Olivia.'

The game resumed. All three of them were deep in concentration. They didn't seem to notice time passing. I shut the door behind me.

Bathtime was over. The kids charged in wearing their pyjamas, their hair damp and worked over with a comb. Olivia followed, floorcloth in hand, and we could eat.

Sitting round the trestle table, we talked of normal things, school, homework, family friends.

Then it was time for a story. I had embarked on *The Three Musketeers*, and then given up, because the kids didn't understand a word, and, what's more, I objected to it. I've never been able to come to terms with Milady's death and d'Artagnan's treachery. Men who smash up everything in their path to gratify their obsession with power and seduction – I already knew plenty of those.

'I think I'm going to go up and get some sleep,' Olivia said, once the children had been put to bed.

'Hang on, first let's have some coffee.'

I could just as well have said to her: Hang on, first let's have a race round the block. Hang on, first let's read the Bible. Hang on, first let's dance a Sardana.

Because I didn't want her to slip off, not yet. I didn't like the idea of her leaving the flat, even if it was only to go to a different floor. I didn't trust the world at all.

What would she do once the kitchen door was closed? Start crying again? Stuff herself with pills? Stare at the ceiling with the radio blaring? Probably all of those things at once, and I wondered how long she'd hold out, how long she could stand it on her own. Courage and strength are not without limits.

It wasn't that I was patient, but I had a sense of duty. We were responsible for all this pain she was causing herself. If it hadn't been for us, maybe she would have kept on taking drugs. She knew the risks and the satisfactions.

But because we were at the foot of the rotten wall she'd been perching on, she'd been prepared to let herself fall, bodily, into the void. Down below, I was running with my arms outstretched. I admired her gesture. I took a sporting approach. I wanted to catch her.

*

'So, what about the babysitter?' Laurent asked as we were talking one day.

'It's fine, it's sorted itself out.'

'She's left?'

'No, she's giving up.'

'Oh. Right.'

He was sceptical. But knowing how difficult I could be, he didn't want to elaborate on his fears and my gullibility. His mistake. I understood perfectly well what he wasn't saying and I sulked for some time on the triple grounds of his withheld trust, stony heart and rank hypocrisy.

As for the dismayed expert, he had his own ideas, but he didn't talk to me about them. I imagine it slipped his mind. He was overcome with lust and consequently took little interest in concerns of a non-sexual nature.

We had been sleeping together for more than two years, and in all that time he hadn't learnt much about my family, my finances or my past. He preferred to guess and make up stories. But I didn't feel disowned by the stubbornness of his ignorance.

Sometimes I'd feel piqued at being treated so unceremoniously, but I also found it oddly attractive. Here at least was one person who didn't know what I looked like with a vacuum cleaner, a shopping trolley or a pen in my hand. I only saw him when I had time to myself and didn't have to account for my life. We didn't talk much. All he expected was a pair of trousers that looked good on me, and a certain ease in the removal of these trousers a little later in the evening.

In the exhausted shambles of my existence, he represented recreation. The restaurant, the hotel and the lipstick. And a little physical activity, when I didn't have time for the swimming pool or the asymmetric bars.

The problem began with my lack of moderation. There came a time when I wanted recreation as and when I liked, perhaps even for ever.

And that was when our points of view parted company at high speed.

I was drinking coffee, sitting casually on the amplifier.

'I can see things aren't OK.'

'Puh,' said Olivia.

'Your sister phoned. She wants you to call back. Maybe you should go and see her, it might do you some good.'

'She's not my sister, she's my half-sister.'

'Do you have the same father?'

Olivia raised an eyebrow.

'Are you kidding? She can't stand Arabs.'

'So?'

'My father's Moroccan.'

'Oh', I said, 'that's why . . .'

'That's why what?'

'Your face. I was wondering.'

She had a heart-shaped face, almond-shaped caramel eyes, pale, delicate skin, a straight nose and thick, full lips. Slightly curly brown hair. A very pretty smile, with white, square teeth.

It had taken me a while to see because of the jeans and polo shirts she always wore. To tease out the likeness, I had to imagine her in iridescent silk pyjamas, with jasmine in her hair and gold chains round her ankles (which was easier said than done). Dressed as an odalisque, frozen in a mildly unstable melancholy, she made a very plausible Sheherazade after her escape from the Little Palace.

From which came her outdated elegance, which was due less to a mingling of blood than of dreams.

From which came my emotional response to her, perhaps, I who had spent so many hours as a child gazing in a giant art book at the heart-shaped faces painted by Ingres.

4

So Olivia had this half-sister called Yvette (who we called her sister) who was married to a guy (who we called her brother-in-law). They had two children, Jonathan and Sophie.

When Olivia and Yvette's mother, a very pretty woman, decided to give up on the recognized world, her children were taken away from her. The neighbours, who had been worried about these neglected kids not being fed or washed, were reassured. The social services might not have a heart, but they did have a head. Under their vigilant supervision, the children would be fed. This much the neighbours were right about.

Yvette was adopted by her grandparents while Olivia was placed with a foster family in Normandy. Their mother, abandoned by both girls' fathers, died of exhaustion. Naturally, because Olivia couldn't stop herself lying, I couldn't guess what she'd left out of her story. Months later I learnt that there was a third sister.

Olivia had never known her father, and had no memory of her mother because she was so young when they parted. She only had a black-and-white photo of her: a picture of a smiling young woman which she had shown me once so I could study the resemblance.

She didn't know her grandparents, either; they had preferred to keep her at a distance, probably because of the Moroccan father – the grandparents had money and a sense of tradition.

*

Olivia hadn't been entirely deprived of family. The social services, in their vigilance, had kept up a tenuous connection between Yvette and Olivia, anticipating that one day the sisters would want to find each other again, to use one another as evidence of their origins. Which was what happened. When Olivia ran away from Normandy for the first time at the age of thirteen, she took the family address with her in her jacket pocket. One fine morning she got on the Paris train. When she arrived, she found her sister's house and rang her doorbell.

'I'm your sister,' she announced to the woman who opened the door.

'Come in,' the woman said. 'We'll see about that.'

Olivia went inside. The die was cast.

The family was reunited. The banquet could begin. Olivia made the coffee. It was her turn.

I first met Yvette when Olivia was moving in. The brother-in-law brought Olivia a mattress and the sister came along for the ride. She was wearing plain, dark clothes and no make-up, and spoke under her breath as if she dreaded the sound of her voice.

She didn't want to come into the flat. She just whispered on the doormat, squinting over my shoulder at the passageway.

'We're half-sisters,' she explained, almost immediately. 'Olivia wasn't brought up by our family – perhaps she's already told you. We're not from the same background, which explains a lot.'

'I'm glad she's come to live with you,' she added, as the brother-in-law went past us lugging the mattress and breathing heavily, Olivia chirping behind him, eyes shining. 'If you knew what she's put us through. It's very good of you to take her. Oh really, what are those two up to? They're taking their time.'

Then the brother-in-law came down, wiping his forehead with a handkerchief. He was a blond, square-shouldered guy, pot-bellied, with thick features and thin lips. He gave me a sidelong look. I thought at first his sight might be impaired, that he might have a sort of multidirectional squint. But he didn't. He just looked shifty, that was all.

They left together, whispering their thanks in a hang-dog way and giving advice, in the form of warnings, free of charge. Then they disappeared, swallowed up by the lift.

'What's up with your sister? She really wants people to know that you weren't brought up together. It's as if she's afraid I'll get it mixed up and think you're the same class.'

'What did she say to you, exactly?'

'Something like, "Oh, we're from different worlds, you know."'

Olivia was ecstatic.

'That's it, that's exactly what she's like. Even before she met you, she had a go at me. You're not going to make a mess, are you, you're going to behave properly. Now you've ended up with respectable people, for once.'

'But she'd never seen me . . .'

'She'd talked to you on the phone.'

'What do they do?'

'They've got this big video shop in Cergy. My brother-in-law set himself up with my sister's money. She's inherited a lot of money, my sister. They've got people working for them. My brother-in-law does some repairs and my sister manages the shop.'

5

Before I'd got a telephone installed in the maid's room, Olivia and I shared the same number. So, for a while, I inherited the calls Olivia didn't want to answer. She gave me drastic instructions.

'Please tell them I'm not living here any more.'

'Can I be unpleasant?'

'If you like.'

I didn't even write down the messages, ferociously breaking off all contact. I just answered that Olivia wasn't here, not any more, no, I didn't know where they could get her, goodbye, please don't call back again, ever.

Sometimes she'd ask me, 'You haven't had a call from a guy with quite a soft voice, quite polite, probably pretty late, say about eleven o'clock?'

And when I said yes and that he probably wouldn't be calling back, she'd smile with relief.

'Good thing too.'

I would have loved the phone to start ringing, right then, that minute, so I could tell another one to go to hell.

But, out of all the calls, I couldn't get rid of the sister's. She was more enraged than anxious that Olivia didn't answer. Without discouraging her definitively, I had been politely but doggedly obstructive. I loathed the woman and her whining voice on the phone.

'I know you don't want to see your sister, but don't you think you should go out for a bit, just for a change?'

'No,' Olivia said. 'It's better if I don't go out too much right now. The minute I step outside the front door, I meet people. Do I look like someone who wants to meet people in the street?'

No, she didn't. She was fat, her hair, which she usually kept in pretty good condition, was in a wretched state and there were bags under her narrowed eyes.

'Well,' I said finally, 'you have put on weight.'

'Don't worry, I've gone up to ninety kilos before. Wait till you see the photo, I'll go and get it.'

The photo had been taken with a flash. The faces were pasty, the clothes lurid and Olivia was enormous.

'I wouldn't have recognized you. You don't do things by halves, do you?'

'I was eighteen. It's weird, isn't it?'

'Yes, it makes you look much older.'

'I know. It wasn't the best time of my life.'

'Do you think you'll put on as much as that again?'

'I hope not. Things'll get better and I'll stop stuffing myself. When I'm well, I lose weight really fast. You'll see.'

'I can't wait for you to feel well,' I said. 'I love it when you're well. The children do too.'

'Do you think they notice I'm not feeling that great?'

'Not that much, but they're bound to a bit. You can see that you're tired and you can feel that it's a struggle.'

'Is that why they're being nice?'

'Not necessarily. They're nice because they love you very much.'

'I love them very much too,' Olivia said.

Before she'd even seen them, with only their names to go on, Olivia had adopted Thomas and Suzanne. I don't mean that she had decided to love them. No, I mean she had taken their side. Against the world and everybody else; me included, if need be.

'Suzanne,' she'd say, 'won't have any trouble coping. I'm not worried about her. But Thomas needs support. You know what they're like in schools, they don't know anything about children. They do kids in completely if you don't protect them. You should be careful. Thomas isn't like the others.'

Olivia's boundless solicitude was confirmed every day, or almost every day, by the disastrous results Thomas brought home from school. Every below-average mark was instantly interpreted as a sign of his exceptional talents.

'The problem,' she'd say, sounding disillusioned, 'is that he's exceptionally gifted. So obviously it's not going to work out well at school.'

She'd be in despair about him. She'd dream of getting him away from the teachers' grubby clutches. Sometimes, early in the morning when I was getting ready to go to work, she would take the children to school and then bring Thomas straight back.

'It's useless him going there. He's bored out of his head.'

It was true that, as far as learning anything was concerned, school wasn't much good to Thomas. He wasn't exceptional in that respect. But he did meet people there. He escaped our anxious love. So I told Olivia that as far as possible and with certain exceptions, I'd prefer him to go to school.

'Maybe,' I suggested, 'he's learning something about the world. Maybe he's learning some form of resistance. For the time being he thinks he's defeated. But we know that one day he'll be the winner, because he deserves to be and because we love him. Olivia,' I concluded, 'we can't always run away. Sometimes we have to stay and fight.'

I shook my fist in the indifferent air. Neither she nor I believed very strongly in our own chances of victory.

6

Winter set in at the start of November. I bought sacks of wood. After supper we'd make a fire and the four of us would sit in front of the fireplace, watching the flames. We'd ask each other questions about heat and energy that we couldn't answer.

One evening we ran out of wood. I realized the sack was empty and tears welled up in my eyes. It was too late to go out for more, the shops were shut. It was cold and rainy outside.

'It doesn't matter,' Olivia said.

'I know it doesn't but it still makes me sad.'

I decided to burn a door which had been cluttering up the box-room ever since we'd moved in and which didn't match any of the cupboards in the flat. As I didn't have a saw we decided to burn the door whole and I wedged the top into the fireplace. The wood was dry and the door caught fire quickly. We spent a lovely, peaceful, silent evening, gently pushing the door towards the back of the fire-place as it disintegrated. The flaking paint caught easily. Little sparks of colour ran along the surface. I tried to work out for a minute where the source of the particular satisfaction there is in burning one's furniture, in one's own home, on a winter evening. Then it came to me.

'We're Bernard Palissy,' I announced gleefully.

'Who's that?' Olivia asked.

'Doesn't matter.'

I poked at the embers. I didn't have that much need for conversation. When the door had been burnt, the evening was declared over. Olivia went upstairs and I went back to my room.

*

That same week, I made herbal tea with thyme, because I'd read in a magazine that it protects the bronchial tubes and stops you getting colds. I watched the stalks infusing in the yellow water. I loved breathing in the scented vapour.

'Try this,' I said to Olivia, 'it's good for you.'

'Mmm,' said Olivia, 'I like the taste, too.'

I was so pleased with this new improvement to our existence that I infused thyme all day long. Herbal replaced normal tea. We drank it non-stop. After several days, Olivia and I became ill.

'I think it's the thyme,' Olivia suggested.

'Yes, we'd better stop. Anyway, if you drink too much of it, you get spots.'

Anything that wasn't excessive didn't interest me. I stopped buying thyme. I felt melancholy. I regretted not knowing how to make use of the world.

Our conversations were usually about drugs. Having come off them for the time being, Olivia had gone to ground in the flat like a terrified dormouse.

'Bread would be nice,' she'd say, 'but I don't feel up to going to the bakery. If you could go, that'd be good.'

She only agreed to go out to collect the children from school.

'I'm scared of running into people I know,' she'd say. 'Knowing my luck, as soon as I poke my head out the door I'll bump into someone.'

'So?'

'So, I'm scared.'

'Scared of what? Are you mixed up in something? Do you owe somebody money?'

'It's not that. It's more that I can't stand up for myself. They'll talk to me, they'll say, come on, it'll be nice – that whole number. I know what I'm like. I can't say no.'

She put her head in her hands and rubbed her cheeks. Her cheeks blushed in patches.

'Sometimes I think I'll never make it.'

She sniffed.

Quarter-past seven. It was time to sit down and eat and we still didn't have any bread. I grabbed my cagoule and raised my voice.

'And why aren't you going to make it? Eh? Because of a couple of delinquents who are hanging around on the street when they should be asleep in prison? Wait a bit while I take care of it. I'm going to the police. I haven't got a record, I earn my living, I've got a family, I'm in my rights.'

Olivia lowered her head and looked at her feet.

'And you're coming with me. Tomorrow morning we're going to bring charges, both of us. Then at last you'll be able to leave the flat. Bloody hell, everybody should be able to walk down the street. Check on the children, will you? I'm going to get some bread.'

'Not the police,' groaned Olivia, scuffing her slippers. 'I think I'd rather cope with this on my own.'

'Alright then. You've only got to say no, after all. It's easy. Watch. NO.'

'But that's just it, I don't know how to . . .'

'Well, learn then, for fuck's sake.'

'Olivia!' shouted the children.

'I'm coming!'

I slammed the door. I ignored the lift. I stormed down the six flights of stairs, taking them four steps at a time.

The baguette was white and gooey.

I laughed as I came back up the street. I pictured us at the police station, me in a middle-class rage, the poor, cynical police, and Olivia standing there, her eyes glistening with recent repentance, like two Chupa Chupps lollipops stuck in the middle of her face.

I didn't turn the light on in the hall. I rang for the lift. As I waited, I chewed the end of the baguette. The curtain of the concierge's flat drew back. Mme Alvez came out, a shadow in the shadows.

'A man,' whispered Mme Alvez, 'came to my flat asking for Mademoiselle Bernier a few minutes ago. Do you know Mademoiselle Bernier's visitors?'

'Slightly,' I said out of solidarity, because no, I didn't know these men, not personally.

Mme Alvez looked at me, perplexed.

'These men,' she went on, 'are gangsters. Perhaps you should ask around, ask Mademoiselle Bernier herself . . .'

The lift came but I was looking at Mme Alvez. I was finding it very hard to understand what she was saying, her accent was so strong and I was studying her so closely as she spoke. Her beauty staggered me, her narrow face in its halo of dark curls. Her slender frame, her black clothes. She wore mourning like a jewel – despite her youth, she was a widow.

I was also slightly apprehensive that, for one reason or another, she'd go to my landlord. When it came down to it, I was a single woman with two children, which made me vulnerable and virtually Poor, or, at any rate, undesirable to the sensitive owners of Parisian flats. Even though I always paid my rent before the fifteenth, each month I half-expected to be given my notice on the grounds of unreliability, or some moral failing.

Mme Alvez wasn't born yesterday.

'I won't say a thing,' she said, 'as long as the other tenants don't complain. But you should be careful. I'll end up getting complaints.'

'Thanks, I will be.'

I opened the lift door.

'I promise,' I added.

Then I ascended gracefully into the air.

Deep down, I trusted Mme Alvez. The children were our bond. Thomas and Manuel, her nephew and godson, had become friends. The two boys were classmates and neighbours, Manuel's mother being the concierge of the next-door building, where she lived with three children and a husband who'd been lamed by an accident at work.

Manuel often spent the late afternoons at our flat, playing with Thomas. And Thomas used to go down to Manuel's to watch videos. I liked Manuel – his politeness, his moon-face and his activities, which were organized by the Portuguese parish church his family belonged to. One afternoon I had taken them to a museum, but neither of them, it turned out, liked museums, and on the way home I had slapped Thomas. Mme Alvez would only denounce me in dire extremity.

By the time I pushed open the door of the flat, I had eaten a third of the baguette and the children were in their pyjamas and doing their homework.

7

While they'd been waiting, Olivia had reassumed her role of primary school tutor, a role in which, with her imperious spelling, her inexhaustible arithmetic and her unlimited patience, she excelled. The only problem was she was too kind.

She was sitting soberly, half buried under an avalanche of paper, indefatigably going over the erroneous results of a decimal division. The child in question, meanwhile, was nuzzled against her hip, reading a *Picsou* magazine and distractedly scouring an old jar of Nutella with his finger.

'You should see what he has to do, the poor thing,' she said, anxiously running a hand over his tousled hair. 'Those teachers are off their heads. But don't worry, we'll be finished in five minutes. Hey, you, pay a bit of attention! I won't always be around to do your maths.'

While I laid the table, Olivia wore herself out deciphering a barely legible photocopied page. That evening we learnt that a King of France had had a wall built round Paris, or round the 11th Arrondissement, or round something, the text wasn't very specific – anyway a wall which hasn't existed for a long time, even as ruins. The wall had been built around about the year 1200 and Thomas didn't know if this considerable event had taken place before or after the dinosaurs became extinct, the one unswampable landmark for him in the floodplains of historical time. As for Olivia, she knew that the extinction of the dinosaurs had preceded the Kings of France, but not much more than that.

More generally, I had been astonished to discover that the name of Marx was unknown to her, as were those of Jaurès, Gutenberg, Chekhov, Roosevelt, Stalin, Baudelaire and Martin Luther King. She knew nothing of this century and its wars. She didn't know who was in the government. History slipped off her like water off a duck's back. There was something beautiful in this inestimable ignorance. At least I thought so, because I loved her. And because I was grateful to her for teaching me that it's possible to live amongst people without knowing their histories.

One day, when I let my amazement show, she said ruefully, 'The doctor warned me, "Olivia, crack cocaine shoots the memory to pieces. It goes, little by little. That will happen to you too one of these days if you carry on." He was right. I don't know anything and that's why.'

I waved aside her regrets with a broad sweep of my arm.

'It's easy to blame it on drugs. The real reason you don't know anything is because no one's ever taught you anything. If you want someone to blame, you just have to say that it's society's fault. And if you want to make up for it, you just have to look at some books, the flat's full of them.'

It was a ridiculous suggestion, of course. Olivia declined politely.

'No, thanks. I've already got too many things to think about. I haven't got room for books. Not now. One day. Later, maybe.'

'You know Armelle?' Olivia asked me one morning.

She was looking with some bafflement at the white plastic shelves where I stacked my books in any old order as they arrived in the flat, always promising myself I would sort them out – even dreaming of cross-referenced filing systems – but never actually getting round to it.

'You know how nice she is? She took me to FNAC one day because I'd looked after her kids. "Come on, I'll buy you something," she said. I didn't ask what. I was just pleased. We got there and I saw books, hundreds and thousands of books. Armelle plonked me down in the middle of the shop and said, "I'm going to choose a book, have a look around and get what you like, it's my treat." She turned around and went off. I was left there, all on my own, and I started crying my eyes out. All the books looked the same to me. How was I supposed to choose one of them rather than another? But I didn't want to stand there like a lemon, so I grabbed any old one from a pile and choked back my tears. We went up to the till. "Oh," Armelle said, looking at the cover, "I'd never have guessed." I never found out what she wouldn't have guessed, I didn't ask.'

*

As far as the wall, the history and the books were concerned, none of it mattered in itself – the point was to learn things off by heart. And Thomas couldn't do it. Olivia gazed at him admiringly, detecting genius in his faraway expression. They were going round in circles. The soup was hot.

'Forget about the wall, Thomas, no one cares,' I said.

'Oh,' groaned Thomas, 'I'm going to get a bad mark again. Anyone can see *you* don't have to go to school.'

'He could just stay at home with me tomorrow,' Olivia suggested.

Suzanne, who was quietly reading a Christmas catalogue that was two years out of date, perked up.

'What about me? Can I stay at home too?'

'No!' I shouted at the top of my voice, to make myself clearly understood, 'Everybody's going to work tomorrow, including children, that's the way it is. Come on Thomas, sit down, we'll start that stupid thing again after we've eaten.'

'It's not fair,' Suzanne muttered.

She complained the whole time. It was one of her qualities, one of the things that made her precious to us, this ability to protest.

After supper Thomas sat on my lap and we reread the photocopy a good dozen times. By nine o'clock I knew the wall like the back of my hand. Thomas, meanwhile, had memorized a few stray words: wall, Paris, saddler. But he hadn't managed to retain the three compulsory syllables: twelve hundred. For a moment I thought of telling him to write them on his arm, as a crib for the next day. But I bit my tongue.

'You already know that this guy, here, Philippe, had a wall built in Paris. That's not so bad,' I observed sympathetically. 'You've got your whole life to learn the rest.'

Thomas appreciated me being loving. He liked it less that I took him for an imbecile.

'Don't always say nice things to me,' he said. 'It makes it worse.'

I took the children to their bedroom and we read a chapter of *Treasure Island* while Olivia did the washing up.

Once the children were in bed and their light was out, there was still the issue of her visitors to raise with Olivia.

'Olivia,' I said, 'there was a guy looking for you just now. He asked the concierge.' Olivia lit a cigarette. 'The concierge doesn't like those guys. I don't either.'

'Oh. Is there more than one of them?'

'Two or three, the last I heard.'

'Oh no,' said Olivia. 'It's my fault. I gave them my address when I moved in with you. I didn't know I'd be staying on here. I couldn't tell, at the beginning.'

Panicked, with a stunned look on her face, she reminded me of the foolish little pig, the one who is celebrating five minutes before the wolf blows down his flimsy straw hut. I swayed my shoulders like the other little pig, the conscientious older one, the cocky owner of a brick house. I know there's something unpleasant about that pig, a sort of conceited self-assurance. But I liked him having a brick house, as protection against the wolf, the winter and Parisian landlords. I identified with him. In a belligerent voice I said, 'Pack up your toothbrush and move in here, on the sofa. They'll soon give up. If they keep on, the concierge will say that you don't live here any more. And if they still don't go away, they'll have me to deal with.'

'Yes,' Olivia said.

'Where do they come from, these guys?'

'It's the rock,' Olivia said.

'I'd worked that out. So?'

✳

Rock. Now that she didn't touch it, Olivia talked about it. She said *rock* the way people say *bike* or *trainers*, because no one can help giving nicknames to their familiar world, to its objects as well as its people. So rock for poorly refined cocaine, and because crack sounded too official. The stuff hadn't crossed the Atlantic before its name arrived, recited by newspapers, picked up by the curious and made unusable for the users – who are people like anyone else, and not too keen on others deciding what labels they should use to describe their environment.

So Olivia had worked for two years in a recording studio, ostensibly as the switchboard operator. The place was full of smokers and run by dealers, which wasn't such a novelty, that era and world were pretty much dependent on cocaine use. She'd felt at home immediately, quite apart from the thrill she got out of bumping into pop stars. The people were nice, dodgy but nice.

'If you knew what a laugh we had,' Olivia would say.

'Right,' I'd murmur.

Out of friendship, all I wanted was to believe her, despite any reservations I might have.

Olivia hadn't taken long to acquire a whole series of subsidiary responsibilities in addition to operating the switchboard. I preferred not to know the details but it became clear she'd been promoted to courier. This gave her the chance to knock on rich people's doors and see for herself what great places they had. Her boss wasn't dissatisfied with her work. Liar that she was, her face inspired a feeling of trust so close to love that she could take the Metro loaded up like a mule – not even the most heartless policeman would have stopped such a fresh-faced girl. The innocence she had written all over her amused them. She could go wherever she wanted, pockets full of gear on the way there and cash on the way back, and she'd look just like a little girl

going home to her mum. And that's where the story really was funny
because that was exactly what she didn't have – a mum. Just rock and
nerve, for sale and to spare. All her friends liked Olivia because you
never got bored with her. She was a really good laugh.

And then one morning the studio went bankrupt, not for want of
business, but through mismanagement or a sudden need to go on holiday, it wasn't too clear. Olivia found herself back on the street. Luck
comes and luck goes. You can always find work again. She did, and she
lost it again. Her friends, on the other hand, she managed to hang on
to.

And now she had to get rid of them.

8

Mme Alvez was enthusiastic about the task of deterring Olivia's pur-
suers. I had conveyed, with broad hints and half-truths, the necessity
of protecting Olivia from herself and her recent past. Mme Alvez had
agreed solemnly. We were very alike, she and I, only too happy to be
assigned simple tasks. Only too happy to interfere in another person's
life, which seemed so accessible when compared to the blurred outlines
of our own.

It was fairly easy to get rid of the pirates who haunted the ground floor
corridor. They must have spread the word. In a few days, the matter
was settled. They went to hell somewhere else. All, that is, except one.

'I just found a note from Sydney,' Olivia said, during one of our
reclusive weeks. 'He put it under my door.'

'What were you doing up there?'

'I was looking for something to wear.'

Out of the whole band of brigands, Sydney, from what I'd gathered, was the worst. The sly one. The cruel one. The nastiest piece of work. To cap it all, Sydney was a *nom de guerre* disguising some nondescript Kevin Dupont with criminal tendencies. But such as he was, he terrified Olivia for reasons whose violence remained obscure to me.

'If you need clothes, just help yourself to mine. You can go back up to your flat when we've finished with this guy.'

That same evening, at about nine o'clock, the bell went. Olivia leapt out of her chair.

'It's him,' she whispered, as if she could see through the closed door. 'I'm sure it's him.'

She started hopping around the dining room like a traumatized frog.

'Calm down, I'll go and see. You take the children to their room and stay there.'

'What is it? What is it?' squealed the children, infected by our sudden agitation.

When they had taken refuge at the other end of the flat, I ran a hand through my hair and opened the door.

Standing on the doormat in front of me, a green bag hanging at his side, was a short, podgy man, with heavy stubble, an affable smile and spiteful eyes.

'Good evening, I've come for Olivia.'

I looked annoyed.

'You shouldn't come here looking for Olivia. She doesn't live in this building any more.'

Sydney watched me, smiling silently. There was something terrifying about his brazenness; I felt that Olivia's fears, whatever they might be, were justified.

'I need to see her.'

'I don't care. I'm telling you that Olivia isn't here, so now you're going to leave nicely and never come back again. Goodbye.'

I thought I'd been unpleasant, but obviously not unpleasant enough.

'As you like. When you see her, you can say that Sydney dropped round and that he's looking for her.'

'I'm not going to say anything at all. Get the hell out of here.'

I slammed the door.

Olivia charged into the passage with the two kids in her wake.

'Oh no, oh no, oh no!' she cried.

Suzanne and Thomas took it up in chorus, clapping their hands.

'Oh no, oh no, oh no!' the flat echoed.

I was assuming a dignified expression, thinking that the Sydney situation had been resolved, when the bell rang again. Several emphatic rings passed through the flat like missiles, leaving a luminous trail hanging in their wake.

Olivia spun round. Realizing there wasn't a way out, she shut herself in the only room with a lock, the lavatory. Thomas and Suzanne followed her, drumming on the door. The door opened, the children disappeared. I could hear them wriggling in their cramped little cubbyhole.

Torn between excitement and hysterical laughter, I dashed into my room, grabbed the Polaroid and went back to the door.

It was the same guy, of course it was the same guy.

'I think Olivia still lives here.'

'Fine,' I yelled. 'You think what you like. But now I'm going to tell you something. If I see you lurking around here again, if you have the nerve to ring my bell one more time, I'm going straight to the police. I don't think they'll have any trouble finding something to pin on you. And if you stay on my doormat another ten seconds, I'll take your picture.'

I brandished the Polaroid. I was ridiculous, he was flustered. He looked at me for a minute, incredulously. Then he turned on his heel and walked away.

'I'll be back,' he called.

I shouted into the stairwell.

'I wouldn't if I was you . . .'

I waited until he was out of sight, then shut the door and put the camera on a bookshelf. I knocked on the door of the safe haven.

'Come out, you loonies. The fun's over. Everyone's going to bed.'

'Already?' asked Suzanne, disappointed.

Sydney's visit was the last episode of the – real or imagined – hounding of Olivia. Two days passed before she moved back into her room. I followed her instructions for a while and continued to give people the brush-off on the phone. Then the calls thinned out, and stopped.

A few weeks later, Olivia said to me, 'Hey, Sydney's been arrested. He'll be inside for a while.'

'Good job too,' I muttered. 'He can stay there.'

Olivia blinked indulgently.

'I wouldn't say that. I can't say that I'm glad. Although when I think about it, I suppose I am, actually. I feel calmer.'

I pouted.

'How did you find out?'

'I met a guy in the street, yesterday. Guess what? They've opened another recording studio, here on the avenue, just past the bakery. Life's funny, isn't it?'

'Quite,' I answered. 'It's quite funny.'

'Don't worry,' Olivia assured me. 'I'm not part of that lot any more. They know that.'

I preferred to believe her. I didn't make a point of it. I said to myself that if she wasn't afraid any more, it was because she no longer had any reason to be afraid.

9

In the evenings, they'd be waiting for me, good as gold, to start supper. Now we were living with Olivia, I didn't have to rush and cut short my meetings in the middle of the afternoon. I felt trusting. My days were longer and my time more serene. I finished work to be back by seven. Often I'd stop on the way to do the shopping.

Olivia hummed as she emptied the shopping trolley I'd just brought back from Franprix. She was putting the things away in an imaginative order. I watched her pensively, smoking a cigarette.

'My God she's fat,' was what I was thinking.

Absentmindedly I felt my hip bone which jutted out like a neolithic tool.

'How can she put on weight so fast?'

I knew she was bulimic. She'd said so, once or twice. But I never saw her eating.

'It's weird, I never see you eating.'

Olivia had finished jamming the cereal packets into the back of the cupboard. She slammed the door. *Chick*, went the magnet.

The cereal was unreachable, positioned next to the boxes of detergent. She turned round and observed me for a minute with a mixture of pity and disbelief.

'Alcoholics: you see them drinking, do you?'

'No.'

There were enough alcoholics in my family for me to know this was true.

'What about addicts, do you see them taking drugs?'

'No, you're right.'

There were addicts too, but not as many.

'Ah, you see? Bulimia's the same. Hard to catch red-handed. You've got to know the signs.'

I nodded. When you want to interfere in other people's lives, you don't have to ask questions. It's enough to watch and wait. Everyone opens up in the end, one day, if you show them enough compassion.

I was lighting another cigarette when the doorbell rang. Suzanne and Thomas rushed to the door, yelling. It was Tuesday evening. Jean-Patrick was coming to pick up his children.

'Dad, Dad!' shouted the children.

'I think it's Dad,' said Olivia.

'Hello Dad,' I said.

Jean-Patrick framed himself in the kitchen door.

'Hi everybody,' he answered, shaking himself.

A ton of water fell off his windcheater.

'It's raining,' he explained, because he never apologized.

'You don't say,' I said. 'You can have supper here. I've just been shopping.'

One of the many advantages you discover after separating for life from a man you have loved for life is being able to invite him to supper with his kids on the spur of the moment.

'It's a deal,' said Jean-Patrick, taking off his windcheater.

The rain made a pool on my tiled floor and I went to get the floorcloth.

*

After supper, Jean-Patrick put on a shadow-puppet display. He stood side-on and formed simple shapes on the white wall of the dining room, which the children identified, jumping up and down. I admired them. They managed to pick out subtle differences between the trembling forms, all of which looked pretty much like rabbits to me.

Then Thomas got up from the table.

'My turn. I'm going to do impersonations and you've got to guess who they are.'

Olivia and Jean-Patrick turned their chairs towards him approvingly. I leant against the wall and crossed my arms, filled with a slight anxiety. I hate shows.

Thomas dropped his usual expression, his dreamy, distant, absent-minded look. He assumed an animated smile, a roguish air, his eyes grew eager. He swayed his shoulders and pretended to chew an enormous wad of gum.

'Don't worry, I got bad marks too . . .'

'Olivia!' yelled Suzanne.

'Not so fast,' said Thomas, 'let the others have a go.'

He carried on. 'You don't have to tell your mother about it straight away. You can just wait for your report. We won't say anything, eh Suzanne, will we? Teachers, they just don't realize how much harm they do . . . Come on, let's go to the bakery and cheer ourselves up.'

'OK,' it was my turn to say, 'it's Olivia.'

I gave Olivia a vindictive look. She was giggling quietly, half embarrassed and half delighted.

'Mum's won,' Thomas announced.

Suzanne rose up in protest.

'What about me?'

'You don't count, it's too easy for you. Right, here's another one.'

Jean-Patrick looked at his watch.

'Alright, but hurry up. It's nine o'clock already.'

Thomas dug his fists into his pockets. He hunched his narrow shoulders and looked down at the floor.

'My God, I'm knackered . . . I've been working all day and I still haven't finished. Hi, you two! Everything alright at school? I've been thinking about you. I bought you some presents. Books. Loads of books. A thousand million books. And not one picture. Not bad, eh? You could at least say thank you . . . Make some effort. Be nice.'

Her hand raised, Olivia got up on her chair.

'Your mother!'

'That's right,' Thomas said.

'I guessed because of the books. When she says that she's got presents . . .'

Jean-Patrick stood up.

'Are we off?'

'Just one last one,' said Thomas. 'Watch closely. Hello mister. What are those bits of string hanging off the end of your shoes? Come on, everyone's going to sit down and do up their laces! Right now! Chop chop! If you're good, I'll take you to the martial arts show . . .'

Jean-Patrick took his windcheater off the back of his chair.

'I know, it's me.'

'Did you get it because of the martial arts?'

'No, because of the shoelaces. Come on, little man, get your back-pack from your room, we're going.'

'See you tomorrow evening.'

'Eight o'clock?'

'Eight o'clock.'

I shut the door on the three of them in their rainclothes, him very tall, them very small. I was always happy seeing them together. It gave me a feeling of peace, a vague sense of achievement which lasted a while after they'd left, like a scent which hangs in the air and then fades.

10

'All the same, you get on well.'

Olivia was clearing the table in a fury of indignation.

'Yes.'

'You don't argue.'

She tipped the ashtray onto a plate.

'No.'

'So?'

'So what?'

'So nothing.'

The glasses screeched. She was stacking them ferociously, one inside the other, regardless of the fragile substance they were made of.

I knew what was annoying her. Slightly after the fact, it was her turn to regret the couple that had broken up. I was used to finding things regrettable. I understood nostalgia.

'Excuse me for asking,' she resumed a few minutes later, 'but why did you two split up? You seem good together.'

I tried a feint.

'I can't marry everybody I'm good with. It wouldn't be legal.'

She persisted.

'Don't you want to answer?'

'Maybe I don't want to, maybe I can't.'

I must have sounded curt, because she looked contrite.

'I'm sorry, I didn't mean to hurt you.'

'It's fine. But I'd be lying if I said I could give you a reason why one day you split up with a man you've known for twenty years.'

'So, you think there's more than one reason.'

'At that stage, they're not reasons any more.'

'You keep on not answering . . .'

'But what do you want, really? Just a sentence to shut you up? Any old one?'

'Yes.'

'Fine, I'll give you one then.'

'Go on.'

'We split up the day I thought that I was going to die if we stayed together.'

Immediately I hated myself for being so pompous. It would have been better to give her grievances. I didn't have to search for long. However much trouble one takes to renew the form, grievances thrive in married life like mushrooms in damp ground. You can always pick them and serve them up in an omelette. Provided you bend down. Search through the mud. Risk being poisoned.

But Olivia nodded. She liked my answer. She was satisfied.

'You see, you did have a reason! That's just what I said to myself, you're not the sort of person who does things lightly.'

I would have liked to talk to Olivia for longer, all evening, if she wanted. But she looked at her watch, stood up and went to open the window. She watched the cars moving along the avenue.

'I'm expecting someone,' she called, shutting the window, which was stiff.

'In this weather?'

It was all I could think of to say. She came back, sat down, and took a make-up purse out of her bag.

'Can I use the bathroom for five minutes?'

I went into my room, to the computer. On my desk, in a grey folder, were two hundred pages a politician had written. He had probably worked at night, or very early in the morning, assembling old enthusiasms, cobbling together new chapters, sewing the whole thing up with rough stitches and at the end adding photocopies of documents that he hadn't had time to condense.

My job was to rewrite this hodgepodge, not to give it any meaning but to clothe it in a form which simulated thought. Once it had a structure, the sentences would follow on from each other smoothly. The eye would travel over them without the idle mind rebelling, absorbed in its ruminative task and finding in the hackneyed mess something like the after-taste of real thought.

The most painful thing was restraining myself from stuffing the text with my personal opinions. Thinking things without being able to have any actual thoughts: the constraint made you mad in the end, and bitter.

I'd never met this man. The work came from a colleague who had a lot of clients and not much time. I was getting 15,000 francs, undeclared. Three little bundles of 5,000, which would materialize as the work progressed. Cash in hand. No business trips. The kind of work you can do at night, when other people are in bed.

Olivia reappeared, her lips brown and glossy, her cheekbones pink, her eyes enlarged by a glittery spectrum of violet tints. I was amazed and momentarily jealous, I didn't know how to put on make-up.

Once again she stuck her head out of the window, checking the street below. Then she gave me a joyful look and slammed the window shut.

'See you tomorrow,' she said, picking up her bag.

She left the flat. I heard the lift descend the six floors.

I didn't ask who she was going to meet, so late at night in the November rain, despite having sworn by the great gods that she never wanted to set foot outside again.

I wasn't very pleased to have been made the dupe of her secrets. But I didn't want to ask her any questions — I wasn't in the mood to swallow her lies.

Nor was I very pleased with her ingratitude. Nor with my own loneliness, now she'd blown me out without any remorse, without the slightest concern that it might be hurtful for me to see her leave and not even be told where she was going or who she was meeting.

'Hello Thierry, it's me. I'm working, I thought it would be nice to have a chat. But you aren't back, it doesn't matter. Call me when you get in, if you like, even if it's late, that's fine, the phone's at the foot of my bed. Anyway, I hope you're well. Talk to you soon. Looking forward to hearing from you.'

I hung up, ashamed of my weakness. But the more my shame grew, the more I wanted to leave other pathetic messages and for Thierry to call me back. I needed some sense of consistency, I felt that I barely existed, diluted by loneliness and waiting.

I went to bed at dawn, when my eyes started fizzing, sending little crackling sparks across the grey screen.

The expert didn't call back, needless to say. I took off my shoes, moved the telephone to the foot of the bed and rolled myself up in the duvet without taking off my clothes. To get to sleep, I let myself think that he was going to call me. He'd probably had to work late as well. He'd be surprised and pleased by my message.

Self-administered lies don't scare me. When it comes to sleep, I'm in favour of any morality that produces results. So I thought, 'My love, my love,' but not for long before I sank into a deep sleep, at one, in my thoughts, with a man who didn't love me. At all.

I I

The alarm went off at seven o'clock. I didn't move a muscle. I counted. Two hours' sleep, if that. No one had called me, they were probably afraid of waking me up. I thought of the children getting up at Jean-Patrick's and realized that I didn't have a meeting that morning. I went back to sleep.

I hoped, as I let myself slip off, that Olivia would wake me up soon, as she usually did; unlike me, she had no trouble getting out of bed in the morning.

She usually made coffee and brought it in to me in bed. I'd cling to my pillow, half-open my eyes and grab hold of the scalding hot bowl. Thomas and Suzanne would come into my room and everyone would sit on the bed and scatter it with crumbs. Olivia would get up, open the window and light a cigarette, blowing its smoke out into the avenue's morning air. Then it was time to get dressed and start: school, work, whatever — something resembling life.

'Shit, eleven o'clock.'

This time I didn't think at all. I jumped out of bed, ran to the bathroom and turned on the bath.

Then I dashed into the kitchen to make coffee.

I had just put the coffee pot on the stove when the back door opened. Olivia came in, half dressed in an enormous grey T-shirt and her slippers and shivering in the biting cold.

'Are you alright?'

She didn't answer. The coffee rumbled in the pot and I poured out two bowls.

As I drank mine, I tried to open my eyes. Despite my efforts, they stayed half closed, picking up only a few rays of light. By holding the bowl under my nose and drinking slowly, the steam gradually unsealed my eyelids. Olivia sat opposite me – white-faced, puffy, her eyes two blood-red slits.

'Oh no,' I thought.

I took back my first words and replaced them.

'You're not alright.'

She didn't answer. I didn't need an answer, I knew what was going to happen. She was going to cry. And that's what she did. She burst into tears.

'No, you're really not alright at all, are you?' I wittered on.

I finished my coffee. Olivia was still crying.

I found it difficult marshalling the necessary words, I'm not very brave first thing in the morning. So I didn't say anything. I waited. I waited for her to stop crying, I waited to find something useful to say, I waited for the world to explode and us with it.

'I want to die,' said Olivia.

'That's not a big surprise.'

'It's horrible,' she continued.

She wasn't listening; it was as if I hadn't said anything.

'It's horrible when you can't bear the weight of your own body.'

'I'll carry you.'

'I wish I'd never been born.'

'That's bloody stupid. What would I do without you this winter?'

'I'm not brave enough to carry on living.'

'Well, too bad. I'll be brave for you.'

'I disgust myself.'

'You don't disgust me.'

'You're wrong. I'm a shit. I should be dead.'

I got up from my chair, threw my bowl into the sink, raised my arms to heaven and yelled, 'THAT'S ENOUGH!'

She shrank down in her chair, put her head in her arms and sobbed.

'Olivia, Olivia,' I said.

I didn't move towards her or take her in my arms, or put my hand on her neck or on her arm.

We never touched, it had become a rule between us. If we happened to brush against each other in the flat we apologized interminably. We never kissed each other hello or goodbye.

Once, when we first knew each other, I'd touched her involuntarily, as a reflex action and because I was generous with physical contact. She didn't recoil. She let me put my hand on her shoulder and graze her cheeks with my lips. But I felt her whole body stiffen. She was revolted.

I had no desire to confront her horror. To transform insignificant rituals of greeting into squalid interfering. I had immediately fallen in with her repugnance.

And I hadn't thought about it beyond that. Physical contact didn't matter that much to me; in the end, distance suited me just as well. But that morning, bathed in tears, the distance felt greater than ever.

I looked at what was in front of me. I saw a girl who had wanted to die since this morning and I tried to think of something we could catch hold of. She'd had dirty hair for several days.

'I've run a bath,' I said. 'Go and get into it.'

'In a minute.'

'Now. The bath's ready. Someone who wants to die can always wash their hair. It's better to be desperate and clean than desperate and dirty.'

'Maybe, but I'm not washing my hair.'

'Why not?'

'When I was in Normandy and Madame Lerouilly washed my hair, she used to put a basin on the kitchen table and make me stand in front of it, completely naked. I had very long hair, washing it took ages. Everyone used to come in and out of the kitchen and they all looked at me. Monsieur Lerouilly used to stand behind me. "What an arse she's got, this one." I can hear him saying that again and again, "What an arse she's got, God, what an arse."'

'So?'

'So, when things aren't going well, I can't wash. It's impossible.'

'I believe you. But we're going to say that it was impossible until today. And suddenly, now it is possible. You've just got to see for yourself. Take a big towel from the cupboard in the bathroom and shut the door.'

Olivia grimaced. She trudged out of the kitchen, hanging her head. I heard the bathroom door slam. I held on to three things. That she stopped crying when she was talking. That the worst was to be expected from a childhood at the Lerouillys'. And that I didn't know what was she out doing last night to make her so sad this morning?

While Olivia had a bath, I began cleaning the kitchen. More precisely, I was seized by a frenzied desire for bleach. I threw cupfuls of it into the sink, on the table and on the floor. I gripped the sponge mercilessly and knelt down on the damp tiles. My hands stung badly but I didn't give a damn. I happily spent a good while scrubbing every centimetre and by the time Olivia poked her head round the door, wrapped up in my dressing gown with her hair dripping, the kitchen was gleaming. The look I gave her was full of hope and tiny triumphs.

'Have you seen how clean it is?'

Two coffees and several cigarettes later, the kitchen was not quite as clean. This constant fluctuation between dirty and clean, bleach and grime is a good lesson for life. A woman who proudly says, whatever she has to do, that it's all in a day's work, isn't any different from a wise man who compares the glory of the path to the vanity of the goal.

As I had hoped, Olivia was calmer after her bath. There was only the sadness left, which came and went like a wave, sometimes lapping at the edge of her eyelids.

I wasn't so anxious to talk about the Lerouilly family again. No doubt they'd return soon enough, trailing calamity behind them. For the moment I didn't have time, I had to go to work. But before I left, I wanted to snare Olivia in a net so fine that she wouldn't be able to slip through and end up alone in a heap on the floor again.

'Olivia, I need you to help me. I'm not going to have time to . . .'

I made a list of shopping we needed urgently that would take her from the post office to the newsagent's and from the grocer's to the tobacconist. I piled crumpled clothes in the ironing basket. Finally I asked her to look in the newspapers and *Pariscope* for activities that would suit Thomas and Suzanne, for Sunday. I wanted us to do something together for once.

Buried under the avalanche of instructions, Olivia agreed, weary-eyed. I sorted out my bag and left, my mind at rest. She'd be occupied until I got back.

In the street, the bracing wind took hold of me, bodily. Under the cotton of my trousers, my legs felt slender and firm. My face grew hot,

then my ears and my hands. I turned up the collar of my jacket. The
expert hadn't called back. But for now, in the cold light of midday, his
silence didn't make me feel so lost. I had comforted Olivia. I had
cleaned the kitchen. I was going to work. I knew I was alive.

12

'Say,' I said to Jean-Patrick that same evening, on the doorstep, 'say I
didn't have any money and I couldn't pay for the flat any more.'

'No problem,' Jean-Patrick answered with a kind smile. 'I'd take the
children.'

'Good,' I said, reassured.

I had a terrible fear of not having enough money to give them
somewhere to live. Of not being able to manage any more. One day.
Soon.

On the dining-room table, Olivia had laid out the shopping in the
order of the list. The ironing was in a pile on my bed and we had three
reduced-price tickets for Sunday's matinee at Reuilly circus. Olivia's
hair shone in the light of the lamps. The morning's tears had dried up.
Sitting in state and wearing her regal slippers, Olivia gazed serenely
round the flat. I bowed reverently to the work she'd done, bending over
double and mentally kissing her fluffy feet.

'What's he do, exactly, Jean-Patrick?' Olivia asked, cutting short my
futile thanks.

'He teaches history and geography.'

She didn't say anything.

'I think he's a very good teacher.'

My word wasn't enough. I tried to come up with some proof.

'He worked at La Corneuve, on the Quatre-Mille estate. Now he teaches at Saint-Denis, in a technical college.'

'That doesn't mean anything. Sometimes they're the worst,' grumbled Olivia.

Olivia hadn't been a bad pupil. She'd been rather gifted and even diligent. School probably suited her, its benevolent discipline and the joy there is in learning. Traces of it remained. Her spelling, always logical if not always correct. The careful way she'd sit down at a table before opening an exercise book, and the satisfaction she took in sorting out a schoolbag. Her ability to add, subtract and understand the rule of three. I would've liked to have found her primary-school teachers and talked to them about the little girl she once was, whom I imagined to be very similar to how she was now, joyful, chatty and hardworking.

Things had turned sour later. At secondary school, she had drowned in the murky flood of knowledge. There wasn't a lifebelt. Even if there had been one, she wouldn't have found anyone to throw it to her. How much time is needed to drive a child to despair? A week can be enough. A month. A year.

Olivia, when all was said and done, didn't do what was expected of her: she gradually stopped going to lessons. Called to order, she was insolent, then insulting. A disciplinary committee followed, and then another one. She was expelled, admitted to another, more distant school. She got a taste of boarding. She tried running away.

She slept in ditches, she stole from supermarkets.

After four years of this, everyone was fed up, Olivia more than anybody. It wasn't that she refused to learn, that hadn't been the issue for a long time. But everyone knew she had lost the war; they were just waiting for her to surrender.

'The headmistress was sitting behind her desk,' she told me. 'The French teacher was standing next to her. Maybe because French was the only thing I was still vaguely interested in.

'"Mademoiselle Bernier," the teacher said to me, "you show no interest in our advice and you refuse to conform to the disciplinary regulations which all your fellow pupils abide by. This school is not here to look after young people who are completely at odds with society. If we had detected in you the smallest, even the *slightest* desire to integrate into the school community, we would have tried — despite the gaps in your education which are immense, insurmountable even. Unfortunately, it's impossible."

'"What is, what's impossible?"

'I didn't want to talk to those two old bags, but there wasn't anybody else.

'"It's not me that's impossible, it's the school . . ." I said to them.

'"Please, don't make your situation worse. The problem, you understand, is that you behave like a madwoman and madness is not something we, I mean the teaching profession, can do anything about, isn't that so, Madame?" She was talking to the headmistress. She wasn't even talking to me, I was nothing, not even a dog, not even a piece of dogshit, nothing. She raised her eyebrows and the wrinkles on her forehead scrunched up into her hair. I started shouting, I didn't know what I was saying. Well, that's not entirely true, I was probably saying things I shouldn't have . . . I admit it, I was screaming.

'"Mad," the headmistress repeated, writing something down in a big book, "completely mad."

'They needed a supervisor to get me out of there. I would have killed her if I could, her or the other one, it didn't matter, I would have drawn blood.

'The thing about it, you see, was that it wasn't really about leaving their horrible school, nobody gave a shit about me there, I completely agreed with them about that. Sorry, it always upsets me when I talk about it . . . Anyway, what the hell, the thing was that my mother was mad. I didn't really know my mother but you've seen her photo, you've seen how I look like her, how she looks like me, and I've always felt that I was like her. When I was very little, I thought that my life would be the same as hers.'

'How do you mean?'

'Well, in one way, wayward, always in love, you know, a pretty woman. In another way, alcoholic. Mad. I don't know if I've told you . . .'

'Yes, you have.'

'What?'

'That she was committed.'

'No, that she was raped by her father . . . Now you see why I've been put off school. They've got the power to destroy you. And they use it.'

'Then what happened?'

'I was thrown out, so I didn't go back any more. I went to Paris.'

'I don't mean that there aren't any good teachers,' she said a little later. 'Just that I didn't have any luck. When I was around, the good ones were busy somewhere else.'

'If you could choose, now, what would you like to do for a living?'

I thought about it. I answered in two parts.

'If I'm thinking about myself, I think I'd like to dig a deep hole, get into it and go to sleep. If I'm thinking about the world, I think I'd like to write books. But it's no good dreaming, I haven't got time, either for the hole or the books.'

'Well, I'd like to be a clown. I think I'd be good at it. I'm good at making people laugh, when I want to.'

Olivia had hung a poster of a clown on the wall of her room. It was an ugly drawing. The clown was sinister. He was crying, naturally.

'Fourteen hundred francs.'

'What's fourteen hundred francs?'

'The course to be a clown costs fourteen hundred francs. It lasts a week. I rang up about it.'

13

I knew that I owed Olivia money. When Agnès sent her to me, that September evening, to babysit for the children – having simultaneously lost her job as a switchboard operator and her flat-share – we had conducted idiotic negotiations.

I was incapable of working out the going rate for the job I wanted her to do: to mind the children after school until I came home, except on Wednesdays when they went to their father's. And I was incapable of putting a price on what I was offering: the upstairs maid's room, on the floor above the flat, which wasn't in a very good state but I promised to have it repainted. I included life with us, a key to the flat, and the meals we had together, but how do you work out how much all that's worth, without knowing the cost of air and daylight too?

Olivia's benefits were guaranteed for another few months. Should we allow for money on top of that? For a travelcard, sure, and cigarettes. But what about money itself: that was the problem, I didn't know how to go about working it out. Do you mind if we start again at the beginning – how much does a room cost? Or else let's do it another way: tell me what you need, I don't want you to go short of anything, we'll come to some sort of arrangement.

I picked up a scrap of paper and a pencil and scribbled down whatever came into my head. Neither she nor I could decide on these two figures: how much a maid's room in Paris costs and how much a babysitter four nights a week costs. Sitting opposite each other on the sofas, we each mumbled ludicrous estimates and then instantly retracted them.

'Tell me honestly, Olivia,' I said, using the polite *vous*, 'how much do you think it should be?'

'Oh nothing,' Olivia shrugged, 'forget about money. And let's call each other *tu*. I'll have the dole for a bit and then I can look for a part-time job, I've always managed to get one whenever I've looked before. Just having a room will be great.'

I chewed my pencil.

'You don't think I'm ripping you off?'

But Olivia wasn't listening to me any more. She got up from the sofa and picked up her jacket.

'Can I come round about seven o'clock with my things?'

'Seven o'clock when?'

'Seven o'clock tomorrow. I haven't got much. Two trips on the Metro and that's it. I'll see about furniture next week.'

She caught me unawares. I would have liked to have thought about it for a bit before I made a decision.

'OK, fine. Tomorrow. And we'll see about the money as we go.'

I'd bring it up every now and then.

'How are you for money?'

'Yeah, fine,' she'd answer.

'Are you sure?'

'Yes, I'm sure. Don't worry.'

'Can you lend me two hundred francs?' she'd say sometimes. 'I'll pay you back.'

And she always did pay me back, tallying up microscopic accounts which I found terrifying in their precision, as someone who never opened their own bank statements and relied on guesswork to appraise the tidal flows of money, its solstices and equinoxes. My awareness of money did, however, extend to knowing when I had some and when there was none left. If the latter was true, being incapable of making cut-backs, I'd increase my workload or borrow from the bank and that way we'd keep our heads above water.

I had a demented hatred of money, compounded of fear and desire. Money was my enemy and I intended to fight. I knew victories and defeats, sudden raids and the wild terror of combat. In the end, I earned my living. But I never experienced a truce, or a peace treaty. The constant confrontations exhausted me. Predictably, I felt as though I was going off the rails.

With the exception of a pair of red bobble knickers, I became con-vinced that Olivia had never bought an item of clothing for herself in her life. People gave her things here and there, as she was passing through – a jersey that turned out to be a size too large, a pair of boots that were too tight.

'To tell you the truth, I don't need anything,' she'd say.

She didn't like spending money, just as she didn't like earning it. She didn't want to have anything to do with it, or as little as she possibly could, needing just enough for bread and cigarettes, and even then she disliked the trade and preferred people to give them to her. It would never have occurred to me that someone as poor as her could shun money to this extent. I also thought to myself that we were alike in this respect and that birds of a feather stick together.

In no time, Olivia's activities had moved beyond the conventional bounds of childcare. When I went out in the evening, she'd babysit Suzanne and Thomas. When the ironing piled up, or the washing-up spilled out of the sink – when everything was covered in dust, including the vacuum cleaner – she'd roll up her sleeves. We never worked out a timetable of household chores. It just depended. Sometimes we were dirty. But other times I got a delicious surprise coming back to a spotless, gleaming flat.

I didn't pay anything for the housework or the rest of it. But I knew it wasn't fair. I was indebted, grateful and embarrassed.

When she told me about the course costing 1,400 francs, I sensed a suggestion of how I could pay her back.

'Perfect. I'll write you a cheque. I owe you loads of money for the ironing, the washing-up, the evenings you've spent babysitting.'

I should have known it was too easy. Olivia turned me down.

'No, forget it. I've got the money. I've already enrolled, for the first week of the Christmas holidays. Don't panic, I checked: the children will be at Jean-Patrick's.'

I was so surprised that for a minute I had a lump in my throat.

'Where's the money come from?'

'There's no need to get stressed. I manage.'

'Nothing stupid, huh? Nothing illegal.'

'I told you, there's nothing to get stressed about.'

We'd had the dodgy goings-on with the tin foil. We'd had the riddle of her night-time excursions. Now we had the mystery of this money. I'm not talking about the thousands of little lies she scattered here and there, out of a sense of aesthetics and a desire for simplicity. I'm just talking about the massive secrets she set down between us, right in the middle of our life together like boulders or trees that had fallen across the road.

'I'm glad,' I said. 'I mean, glad about the clown course. It's a very good idea.'

'Yes,' Olivia agreed, exactly as if I was talking about someone else. 'I think it's good too.'

'But I'm scared you'll do something silly for money. I'd rather you asked me. I'd rather pay you properly. It would be simpler.'

'I'd rather you didn't. Let me do it.'

That evening I issued an invitation to dinner. I called my brother and left a message on his answering machine. Then I called back an hour later. I wanted to read him a little poem by Ronsard but the answering machine cut me off on the third verse.

Soon after that I abandoned the idea of doing any work. Tomorrow, I told myself — tomorrow — over and over again. I lay down. I didn't have a chance to say a prayer. My cheek had barely touched the pillow before my eyes shut gratefully.

The phone woke me at half-past twelve. It was the expert.

I kept my head. As was our habit — steering clear of feelings — we decided to meet up on Friday evening, at a restaurant.

His hours suited me. He was happy to work late. I didn't have to cheat Suzanne and Thomas out of my time to be with him. They'd be fast asleep when I went out and left them with Olivia.

I found it hard to get back to sleep. Between friendship and children, money, work and love, I wondered how people found any time to rest.

In the early morning I dreamt that I was on the set of a pornographic film. An insect with a black shell — half cockroach, half beetle — was lying on top of a young blond woman. It was a wide shot, the two bodies were clashing violently, the insect's black, glossy carapace, the young woman's delicate, pinkish skin. There was something very beautiful, terrifying and erotic about it.

Startled awake by the excess of emotion, I prayed to the Lord to spare me any more exhausting dreams that night. I drifted off to sleep again without any trouble.

14

There were highs and there were lows but there were no more catastrophes. The ups and downs, the truths and lies all passed easily through the silky filter of everyday life. By and large, things were going better. If she hadn't yet lost weight, Olivia had at least stopped putting it on.

I monitored her intake of tranquillizers. I kept an eye on the symptoms. For a while I was worried about her eyes being too dark, her fragile moods, the way she'd suddenly fall asleep.

'You should be careful about what medicine you take,' I reminded her one evening when she looked exhausted and her eyes were vacant.

She seemed sad. I was concerned. I could cope with despair, but sadness made me feel helpless.

'Stop worrying,' Olivia said. 'I've heard it all before.'

Whether she'd heard it all or not didn't make any difference. I didn't like it.

She'd fall asleep for no reason, at odd times, all over the flat, a little walrus out cold on the corner of the sofa. Suzanne and Thomas would respect her sleep. They'd play nearby, seeming to watch over her.

At the time they made a pretty picture. But I'd have been just as happy if she stopped taking so many pills.

'I've got nothing against prescription drugs,' I began one morning, when it was just the two of us alone in the flat.

'Me neither,' Olivia replied slyly.

She looked at me curiously, without a trace of anxiety.

'When they're needed, of course,' I went on. 'I think that you do need them, at the moment.'

'Yeah.'

Standing in front of me, she waited to see what I was driving at.

'Alcyon,' I said casually, as if I was completely changing the subject, 'is total crap.'

A brief smile crossed her face. Then she frowned.

'I get that feeling too,' she whispered.

'At first it helps you sleep, but then it drives you mad.'

'What sort of mad?'

'Raving mad. Paranoid. I don't think someone who looks after children should take it. Because of the risks. Not so much for them personally, but for the children.'

'Do you really think it's dodgy if you're looking after children?'

'Yes, I really do. Everyone says so.'

'But what about if someone's very tense and can't sleep. She has to take something to get some rest. If she doesn't have any Alcyon, what does she do?'

'She asks her doctor to prescribe a less toxic tranquillizer.'

Olivia thought in silence. In conclusion, I said, 'If you ever need something to get by, I've got some Lexomil. In the bathroom cupboard, top shelf. You can just help yourself.'

That was the end of the discussion. And the end of sleeping in the day as well. Maybe Alcyon wasn't involved. But something shifted; whatever it was, it didn't matter. The box of Lexomil took a hammering – that was the tangible sign of change.

My cowardice leads me, as a rule, never to tackle a problem head-on. I prefer defeat to confrontation. I belong to the roundabout school of doing things. This inclination to duplicity proved to be the best tactic for dealing with Olivia. She was allergic to conflict as well. Frank discussions got us nowhere. She wouldn't listen.

Things had to be negotiated. Initially, I'd talk and my words would seem to get lost in a quagmire of indifference. 'Yes, yes,' Olivia would murmur, looking annoyed, clearly thinking of other things. But then, more often than not, my little speech would come boomeranging back to me, quoted as the advice of an old friend. She'd trot out word for word what I'd dished up the day before.

The most efficient method was to erect a screen of generalities behind which the specific issue could be dealt with. The more concrete the subject, the safer we were behind the screen.

'Imagine someone who's very unstable and has been taking drugs for years . . .'

'Mmm,' Olivia would say, and she'd cup her face in the palm of her hands, her chin jutting towards me, her lips pinched in concentration.

'Well, this person . . .' and I'd continue.

At the end of the conversation, Olivia would sometimes say, 'You'll laugh, but that reminds me of myself.'

As I made the stories up, I couldn't help identifying with my heroine and her thwarted progress. She resembled me in more than one respect.

At the start of December, *Greystoke*, a film based on the Tarzan story, was on television. I liked the actor's louche expression, his slight squint, his expressive cries and his misunderstood anger. I was touched by family tragedies, and I felt affection for the great apes. And I was very struck by the idea that parents, who are innately sympathetic creatures, could be chimpanzees as well. I had tears in my eyes all evening.

Suzanne and Thomas, on the other hand, were only moderately moved. They were more interested in whether the monkeys in the film were real, or just actors in suits. They tried hard to distinguish those which were probably real from those that were definitely fake. Throughout December I'd shamble up and down the passage pretending to be a monkey. I'd grunt affectionately, the children would jump on my back and hang on to my neck. I adored feeling their weight on my shoulders. We rolled around, head over heels, laughing.

The date of the clown course was getting nearer. Whenever Olivia spoke to us now it was with outstretched arms, in ringing tones: '*Hel-lo*, children!'

Suzanne, Thomas and whichever kids were visiting the flat after school all adored her clowning.

I had to keep my mistrust of clowns to myself. Whiteface clowns, Redface clowns – the fact is that everything to do with the circus depresses me. Even as a child I'd steer clear of big tops and the wretchedness that blossoms under canvas, parading about and making a spectacle of itself at the first opportunity.

Coming home one night, I stumbled over a pair of clown's shoes left lying on the doormat. I got used to tidying away the red plastic noses forgotten on chairs or wedged down the sides of the sofa, tucking them into the kitchen drawers.

Olivia was summoned to an introductory session. She returned full of enthusiasm. At supper, she haphazardly outlined the various theories of clowning. It should be understood, once and for all, that the clown is not just some guy who makes a fool of himself to get a laugh, but the representative of a demanding and complex discipline which is just as valid as painting, classical dance or biblical exegesis.

She brought back new friends. We grew used to seeing them filing in and out of the flat over the following weeks. Endearing young girls, nerdy young guys, a few deadbeats with time on their hands, prodigious hashish smokers and small-time crooks. She grew fond of the last. She had a kind of intuitive, unconscious gift for choosing utterly unreliable people as her friends.

One evening, when she was running through a repertoire of the different kinds of clown in front of Thomas and Suzanne, the telephone rang. I got up from the sofa where I'd been sitting watching the performance.

'Hello. I'm sorry to disturb you. It's Yvette, you know, Olivia's sister . . .'

I looked through the glass door of the living room. Olivia was bearing down on the dumbstruck children with a strange lopsided shuffle. She leant towards them waving her arms exuberantly. Her eyes were open wide and her face was a mask. She looked like someone, yes, that was it, she reminded me of Annie Fratellini the clown.

'I'll see if she's still here,' I answered coolly.

'Olivia,' I called. 'It's your sister. Do you want to talk to her?'

Olivia froze. Her arms dropped to her sides. Thomas and Suzanne turned to look at me, astonished.

'I can say you're not here . . .'

Too late. Olivia walked, hollow-eyed, towards the phone. She pulled the glass door shut behind her.

'What's happened?' asked Thomas.

'Nothing,' I answered. 'Her sister's on the phone.'

By the time Olivia returned to the living room I'd begun a story. She didn't resume her performance.

'Tomorrow,' she said to the children. 'I'm not up to it tonight.'

15

'Not bad,' said Cécile with an admiring whistle.

I considered myself lucky to be one of Cécile's friends. I was proud of the attention she gave me: she didn't have a reputation for being nice.

I took a sugar lump out of its wrapper and balanced it on the rim of my coffee cup.

'Yes, but I work a lot.'

'Even so,' Cécile continued dreamily – no doubt she was dreaming about her own overdraft. 'Twenty thousand's not bad.'

'I've got to earn that: the rent alone is almost nine thousand.'

'Well, you're doing it.'

It was early and I was barely awake. I felt a surge of vanity.

'I can do more.'

'A lot more?'

'Yes, some months a lot more. Anyway, never less.'

'You're doing well.'

I stirred my spoon in the cup and the coffee swirled proudly. Basking in Cécile's unexpected approval was all very well, but I couldn't enjoy it for long.

'What I do is useless. I write bullshit. It tears me up, thinking of all this time spent on bullshit, all this money spent on bullshit.'

Cécile shrugged. 'Why should you care?'

'It's draining. I don't like what I do.'

'What, and you think other people like what they do?'

'Probably. A bit. Enough. They have to. Or maybe they don't work much.'

'Yes,' she said. 'And because they don't work that much, they've got time to go windsurfing.'

'Parachuting.'

'Visiting the country house.'

'Shopping at Carrefour.'

'Getting depressed.'

We laughed, but there was nothing to laugh about really, either for other people or for me. It was all such a waste.

Then we talked about men. The men we were sleeping with. We made fun of them, cruelly, and of ourselves. We laughed some more. It wasn't any funnier.

'That flat's too expensive for you,' Vincent had said to me, one night in August.

We were coming back from a restaurant. It was a warm evening, his wife was on holiday and we were going to sleep at my place. We were walking side by side on the pavement, pushing our bicycles which meant we couldn't hold hands. It was just before my bike was stolen.

I hadn't taken his remark badly. We'd only recently met up again, and after all those years of not seeing each other I felt a fondness for him that was close to adoration. He had a calm voice, calm eyes, calm hands. He was sensible. That was probably the reason for my adoration.

'It's expensive but it's beautiful,' I'd admitted, a little swayed by his certainty.

'Of course,' he'd said, mollifying me. 'But for the same amount of space, a few kilometres out of Paris . . .'

I'd smiled and closed my ears. I couldn't care less about how much it would cost me to live somewhere I didn't want to live.

'No, no,' I'd sung, 'no suburbs, only Paris. The thing is, I don't need furniture, or clothes, or holidays, or a car. But I do want to like the rooms I live in, the bedroom I wake up in, the streets I walk in.'

'Fine,' Vincent had conceded.

He liked me being capricious and unruly. Because of his calmness, I suppose – I acted as a counterweight.

'After all, with a bit of luck, one day you'll find an old flat round here that's not so expensive.'

Our handlebars collided. I knew I never had any luck, when it came to flats.

We chained our bikes together against a bench on the avenue. Before punching in the entry code for my building, I looked up at the sky, staring into the saturated red Parisian night. I took a deep breath of the good city scent, its mineral smell. Then I searched in my bag and took out my cigarettes. Vincent didn't smoke. He shook his head. He was so often both disapproving and thrilled.

After my coffee with Cécile, I dived into the Metro. I glanced at the wall clock above the ticket barrier on my way down. I was almost early.

Half an hour later I was looking out of a seventh-floor picture window at the grey sky, the grey roofs, the timid, dirty light and its blue-tinged reflection off the zinc. I took a felt-tip pen out of my jacket pocket and moved the ashtray towards me.

Holding a cup of coffee in each hand, Jérôme pushed open the door of the meeting room with his knee. He smiled and I wondered what it would be like to sleep with him; on a weekday, at the Mercury at the end of the street, say.

'Down to work,' he said with gusto.

'Down to work,' I repeated, a tone lower.

✢

I had to be careful not to stare at Jérôme. His face was covered with patches of red, dry skin. He was sloughing, like a snake basking on a rock. For a guy who spent his days and nights in the office, and not in the sun, it didn't seem fair.

I was dying to ask him about the disastrous state of his skin, but I couldn't. Relations between us were friendly, but recent. They stopped at the door of the agency. He would have misunderstood, he'd think I was making fun of him. That I was pitying him. That I was coming on to him, even – he was conservative, a Catholic. 'It makes sense you getting eczema,' I wanted to say to him. 'I can't imagine you getting depressed.'

'So,' Jérôme said with a childlike smile, which disarmed any attempt at serious conversation. 'Don't you think it's an interesting project?'

I didn't think the project was the slightest bit interesting. What I thought was interesting was the money. But like everyone he wanted a show of love, so I gave him one – you have to know what you want, and I wanted to work.

'It's an excellent idea.'

Respectfully, I weighed up the file he'd just put in my hands.

'We're going to be able to do something really exciting.'

'Yeeees!' Jérôme said approvingly.

He was happy. Pleasure etched a little arc of lines round his eyes.

'That's what I thought. Some proper research, something really intelligent. I thought of you immediately.'

I put the file down on the table.

'Jérôme, you're an angel. I love working with you.'

There was nothing to be proud of: that's how I am with people who give me work. They're usually so aware of the vanity of their occupation that they need you to comfort them. You can embroider their own words, sparing yourself any great rhetorical effort. A good show of affection does the job perfectly well.

I spread the pages across the table in a friendly way.

'I'm all yours. Off you go, I'll take notes. Tell me exactly what you want.'

I was no longer young enough to believe that love was what the clients really wanted as their full and final payment. What they really wanted, all of them, was power and money and the innumerable pleasures you can treat yourself to when you've got these things. You only had to listen to them talking once they'd opened up and forgotten themselves, and they appeared for what they really were, cynical – or perhaps cynical and unpleasant.

And yet, mystery of the human psyche, before they enjoyed their rewards, they also wanted love. And admiration, and trust, enthusiasm, intelligence, respect for their civic-mindedness and a sense that you shared their dreams – they wanted all these things in addition, and they wanted them for free. That was the deal, and so I pretended.

I'd had it up to here with work.

By the end of the morning, I was satisfied, calmed by the prospect of pocketing a good wad of money when the work was finished and the accounts department had been notified.

Jérôme possessed an archaic kind of honesty: he paid for the work that was done without moaning about the agreed price or fiddling things so as to cut his overheads. He offered advances. This was so rare that, even when I calculated the profit he must be making off me, I didn't feel inordinately resentful.

*

I'd finish my work at weekends or at night.

I'd put the children to bed, doze, for an hour or so, open-mouthed, on the sofa, and then get out my papers. 'Are you still working?' Olivia would ask.

'Yes, there're fewer distractions at night.'

I'd put on some music and switch on the computer. Olivia often stayed, hanging about and constantly interrupting with comments on the day's minute events.

'Shall I make you a cup of coffee?'

I was grateful for her being there to witness my efforts. Thanks to her, what was just a sort of contemporary con trick took on the aspect of an epic. I was no longer just a divorced, spendthrift, disorganized woman, but the heroic captain of a ship in a storm.

'What do you do, exactly?' people would ask.

I'd hesitate, then mumble.

'Loads of things.'

I'd give them a haphazard list: articles, surveys, studies, dossiers, brochures, reports, educational materials, research. Lay-out. Publishing. Proofreading. Everything I've learnt how to do, I do. If I don't know how to do something, I can learn. It depends how much they're willing to pay me. And as long as I don't have a boss sticking his nose in my diary and checking up on what I do with my time.

If I avoid nine-to-five, I'm not completely unhappy. I had a go at that when I started and I still regret it. While it's possible, I don't want to sell my life. My life is mine. I prefer to sell my work. While it's possible, of course.

16

Olivia was lying on the floor, leafing through the newspaper. She stopped at the TV supplement.

'Hey!' she exclaimed, half sitting up and turning towards me. 'Hey, look! I know her.'

I screwed up my eyes. I couldn't make the person out, the photo was too small.

'Who is it?'

'Don't you recognize her? Karen Cheryl!'

'The singer?'

She sat up with the supplement open on her knees and read the article under the photo.

'She's really nice, you know?'

Olivia's knowledgeable tone marked a gulf between us.

'It was when I was working as an assistant to Dany, the press officer at the record company, remember, I told you about that . . . She used to take me along to interviews. We went to Karen Cheryl's, to her house. She even gave us a drink. And can you believe it, it makes no difference to her, being Karen Cheryl. She's *really* unhappy. It's mad, isn't it?'

'No,' I said. I was absorbed in copying out my address book.

'What?'

'Yes, I mean, yes it's mad.'

'Karen Cheryl, Karen Cheryl,' Olivia repeated, her voice full of nostalgic admiration, possibly for Karen but more likely for the old Olivia, the Olivia who had met her.

'When I was twelve, I spent a whole winter dreaming about meeting France Gall. I'd heard one of her records at a friend's house.'

'But I'm not talking about France Gall,' Olivia corrected me curtly. 'I'm just saying I know Karen Cheryl.'

I picked up my pencil and waited for her to say more. But she gave me a pitying look and left it at that.

I had a meeting at three o'clock. It took me half an hour to find the front door of the flat, which was hidden at the rear of a paved, tree-lined courtyard, up a spiral staircase nestling among branches, at the end of a panelled corridor.

'You'll see, he's adorable,' Nathalie had said to me. 'He's looking for a researcher for a TV project. I told him about you.'

He was adorable. He was also minute, swallowed up at one end of a vast sofa which could easily have accommodated fifteen people his size.

A younger man with dark hair was perched on the back of an equally vast sofa, facing him. He was playing with a pair of smooth, shiny chrome balls, rolling them rapidly between his fingers. No doubt this was meant to show that he was a magician, or that he was giving up smoking, or perhaps both.

'Nathalie has told me a lot about you,' the small man began.

His voice didn't carry well in the dark, cluttered space. It idled on the mezzanines and then trailed away.

Balanced at the other end of the sofa, I was trying to get out of my jacket.

'I'm working on a project about the recession. A drama.'

'People having a hard time,' the young man carried on, picking up a recalcitrant ball. 'I'm the scriptwriter.'

'Yes, so we're looking at two leads . . .'

'Or three.'

'Or even five – basically a bunch of friends who find themselves in the shit. *La Belle Équipe*, you know? They're unemployed, not entitled to benefit any more; or maybe they've never actually been in work, no money – you get the picture?'

I took out my notebook, nodding vigorously.

'We're thinking of a series. I want to write about all the scams those sort of people come up with. How they get by, deals they pull off – you know what I mean. The idea is to make a funny series set during the recession.'

I nodded again. I wasn't sure what to write down. I drew some circles in the margin of my notebook.

'We'll need research.'

'On having a hard time?'

'Yeah, on the little rackets they've got going. Those guys are bound to get up to stuff . . . That's the stuff I want.'

I scratched my forehead.

'Moonlighting?'

'No, not work. They haven't got any work.'

'The job centre?'

'No, not that either. I'm not making a documentary. I'm making a TV drama.'

The guy may have been adorable, but I couldn't see what he was driving at.

'Well, there's drug-dealing, but I don't see how to make that funny,' I said.

'I'm going to stop you right there,' the young man cut in. 'We're working for TV. There are some things we can't show. Drugs, for instance. They're a no-no.'

'No prostitution either.'

'No stealing.'

'And no foreigners. No one black, at any rate.'

'Nothing shocking. Nothing bitter.'

'We want light, funny. Contemporary. Hopeful.'

'That's right. Hopeful.'

The room was filled with a sweet smell of incense and Dutch tobacco. I thought to myself that the young man must be the adorable guy's son. I thought to myself that you can always come up with research material. I thought to myself that the series would never get made.

'It won't be easy,' I said, 'but I'll do my best.'

Time was passing and I was trying to gather up the sleeves of my jacket when the adorable guy stopped me with a wave of his arm.

'Now, about money . . .'

I got ready to protest, to put off negotiations till later.

'I'm offering twenty-five thousand francs. Half now.'

Twenty-five thousand. Suddenly I felt very hot. I could feel myself flushing.

'I don't know if it's worth that.'

'That's what we've decided. The contract's ready. Sign it on your way out.'

'No drugs?' Olivia said, intrigued. 'What then — booze?'

'What are these guys thinking?' was her next question.

'Still, you may as well have a laugh about it,' she said a bit later. 'No point in being too sensitive.'

I crossed my arms on the table and laid my head on them.

'But where am I supposed to find a guide to poverty?' I groaned. 'At the town hall?'

'If that's all that's worrying you, calm down, I've got what you need.'

Olivia kept a box file among her things. In this file were sheets of squared paper on which she'd neatly written down addresses. Dozens of addresses. Where to find clothes, shoes, food, a bed, a shower. Public baths, hospitals, psychiatric departments, rescue centres, social services – in the suburbs and the arrondissements of Paris – the Salvation Army, Emmaüs, La Mie de pain, Marmottan, African workers' hostels.

Along with the addresses were leaflets about healthcare cards. Emergency benefits. The different departments of the DHSS.

'I'll lend it to you,' she offered. 'You can give it back to me later.'

I gathered together the documents and closed the file reverently.

'Olivia, do you want to have a work meeting with me tomorrow evening, after supper?'

'What sort of work?'

'You tell me things that happened to you when you were on the streets and I'll take notes.'

'Yeah, sure. If you're interested, I could go and see the counsellors at the Job Centre and social services. That might be helpful.'

'OK. But let me pay for the clown course.'

'No.'

'Fine, I'll pay for the next one.'

'Do whatever you feel like.'

There were the old ladies she lured into alleys so that her friends could rob them.

There was the stealing – shoplifting, bag snatching, pickpocketing.

There were the squats.

There were the drugs that they bought, stole, cut and sold.

There were the fights, beatings, and settling of accounts.

There were the psychiatric hospitals.

There were the people who poisoned themselves on purpose so that they could have a nice sleep in Casualty.

There were the girls you don't see on the street because they manage to find a guy every night and never have to sleep rough.

And then, fortunately, there were the real friends, the ones you didn't dare let yourself hope you'd see again and then one day happened to run into. You concealed the lousy state you were in. They welcomed you in. You moved onto their sofa. You got yourself back together.

But then, unfortunately, vice and drugs and friends would come round again and you'd end up back on the street, involved in all sorts of dodgy goings-on, up to your neck in it.

Nothing, absolutely nothing Olivia told me was usable.

'What about your sister?'

'You must be joking. She didn't want to see me. She wanted to pretend I'd never happened.'

'And the social services?'

'I went to juvenile court at one point. I didn't have a choice. The judge gave me a hard time. He was right, really. What's a judge supposed to do with a kid who's decided to go completely fucking mad?'

'How long did it last, this mayhem?'

'A year, two years. It happened in phases. I kept going to pieces, I couldn't help it. I calmed down when Momo took me in. I lived at his place, above his fruit and veg shop. I really liked Momo, I really did 'ike him.'

Momo was at least fifty. She talked about him fondly, how he was kind and patient, how he was a Muslim.

Then Momo had gone back to Morocco. She'd ended up in a hostel at Aubervilliers. 'The bad thing about the hostel was the drugs and the same old stuff, the rapes.'

I'd stopped taking notes a long time back.

'What do you mean, rapes?'

'You know. Rapes.'

She'd never said anything to me before about rapes. And this wasn't the evening for us to talk about them. I'd heard as much as I could bear.

I stood up.

'Let's stop. That's enough for this evening.'

I went to the kitchen and got the vodka out of the freezer.

'You won't forget to give me back my file, will you?'

'I promise. A vodka and then bed?'

'Can I sleep here tonight? It's late – I can't be bothered to go upstairs.'

'Sure.'

I put two glasses on the table. I looked at her in alarm. I'd come so close to losing her before I'd even known her. Rapes. Of course. I was such a fool. What did I think had happened to her?

17

The day had started badly. On the kitchen table, I'd found a page from an exercise book with a few lines, illustrated with flowers and hearts, in Suzanne's hand, who, at the time, was a poet.

> *I can't tell you my sadness*
> *But you seem to me as strong as a poo.*

I'd picked it up, taken it into my room and put it in a desk drawer with the others. I reread the last one.

> *Work well, my little chipmunk.*

Then I sat down on the bed. Discouragement seized me, squeezing hard enough to crush my ribcage. I wasn't worthy. I thought about crying. I thought about going to sleep. I thought about the hole I could dig and get into.

I thought about drinking some vodka and moaning, but I couldn't right then. In a little while, when the meeting finished, I'd have a few cognacs in a café. I wanted to fade into the background. Lose track of myself. Die.

I didn't want to die forever. I wanted to die for six months, a year. Just for long enough to recover.

It was getting late. I stood up, picked up my bag and left the flat.

Outside the building, Mme Alvez was sweeping the pavement. At the sound of the door, she broke off and came towards me. I liked her navy-blue- and black-striped apron a lot.

'Do you know about the bailiffs?'

She took me into her flat and gave me a bundle of registered letters and distraining orders. They came from a credit company and they were all addressed to Olivia.

I stuffed them in my bag, thanking her effusively. She smiled. She had the soul of an accomplice. If I'd ever been a member of a resistance network, I would have liked to have worked with Mme Alvez. We could have hidden guns in her flat. Pamphlets in her apron. She was made in the heroic mould – it was obvious. Her uncompromising beauty. Her tragic face. Her youth.

I went off to the Metro, the bundle of letters weighing heavy in my bag. I wasn't feeling so sad any more. Instead, I was furious.

An interview and two cognacs later, rather than going to the agency and finding a lunch companion, a freelance at a loose end who I could have talked shop with over an omelette, I decided to go home.

The air was cold and dry, the light harsh, the empty flat flooded with sunshine. I didn't stop to take off my jacket. I sat down on the floor and took the letters out of my bag. Then I picked up the phone. I had no problem getting hold of the person I was looking for.

'I couldn't give a damn about what she signed. You can take your schedule of repayments and you can stuff it. She's not paying anything back. And since she hasn't got anything, there's nothing for you to take. No, excuse me, I don't owe you anything at all. I'm not her mother, she just stays in my flat. Free of charge, yes. And you can stop threatening me or I'll set my lawyer and the consumer rights people on you. What's not in order is lending money to kids, that's what's not in order, it's your hard luck. Goodbye, Madame. And the same to you.'

And, click, I hung up. And glug, glug, I poured myself a vodka. Someone had to finish the bottle.

I waited for her to come back. I turned on the computer and dozed in front of the screen, congratulating myself on my show of authority.

'Hey, are you back already?'

Olivia popped her head round the door.

'Sit down, I've got something to say to you. Do you remember borrowing money from anyone?'

Olivia looked at me with eyes full of righteous indignation.

'I don't owe anybody anything. You know what I'm like with money. Even if it's fifty francs, I pay it back. It's other people that forget to pay *me* back.'

'You lend money, do you?'

'Sometimes, when I've got it.'

'Who to?'

'Jean-Michel, for example. The guy in the hat, the one I met on the course. I lent him eight hundred francs to move house, but he didn't move, in the end. I think he smoked my money, actually.'

'What are you talking about? Some guy rips you off eight hundred francs and you laugh? You idiot! At least stop laughing about it!'

'I can't help it if it makes me laugh . . .'

'Right, so you don't owe anyone any money?'

'Hang on! I don't owe any *people* any money, I owe *companies*. I owe the electricity board two thousand francs. But that's from a long time ago. And it wasn't even for me, it was for Momo, for the shop.'

'No one cares who it was for. Go on. The electricity board's it, is it?'

'Telecom.'

'How much?'

'Wait, I'm trying to remember . . . thirteen hundred, I think.'

'*What?*'

'It was when I was living in Pigalle with some Africans, the line was in my name. I won't tell you what a state I was in then. Everyone took advantage. The Africans phoned home so often they practically went deaf. Luckily Telecom cut us off in the end.'

'Luckily. Telecom and the electricity board. Is that it?'

'We're not counting fines on trains and the Metro?'

'No.'

'Then that's it.'

'Right. It's hard luck on the electricity board, they shouldn't have lent you money. But you should go and see the people at Telecom. If you tell them a sob story, they'll work something out.'

Olivia grimaced.

'It wasn't me who made all those calls and ran up the bill . . .'

'Still.'

'Why are you so worried? Is it because my line's in your name now?'

'I'm not telling you because it's an issue now. I'm telling you because it'll matter later. When you have a flat in your name, you'll need a telephone in your name to go with possessions in your name and a cheque book in your name.'

Olivia didn't answer. She looked at me with a pained expression. She obviously thought I wanted to throw her out.

'Not now,' I said to reassure us both. 'One day. Later.'

18

'How old are you exactly?'

'Twenty-three.'

'What sign are you?'

'Libra.'

'So . . .'

'Yes, it's in a week.'

'What day?'

'Tuesday.'

'Excellent. We'll celebrate. Who do you want to invite?'

Olivia picked up the newspaper and tore off a corner of a page. She rolled it into a cone and spat her chewing gum into it. She looked perplexed.

'You won't have to do anything. I'll take care of dinner and you can think of who you want to invite. I'll make the calls.'

'Have I got to tell you now?'

'No, tell me tomorrow. But not later than that. It takes time to get hold of people.'

Olivia was lost in thought all evening.

'Are you sure about my birthday?' she asked before going up to her room.

'Yes.'

I like birthdays. I've got into the habit of celebrating them. No matter what state the kitchen's in I can always find the little paper bag with the half-used blue and pink corkscrew candles, which I bring out all year round. It's not that I like buying presents. I find sending out invitations annoying, and it's boring ringing people up. But let's face it, if it wasn't for birthdays how would we know that we're here and that our days are numbered?

'The children will be so pleased,' I added.

That was a low blow. As I'd anticipated, Olivia conceded the fight.

'I'll play with the children,' she said compliantly.

Next morning, braving her reticence, I asked Olivia again for a list of the people she wanted to invite to the dinner in her honour.

'Your sister and brother-in-law?'

'No, no . . . Let me think.'

My suggestion acted like a threat. As if to ward off Yvette, Olivia started scribbling feverishly on a scrap of paper.

I went and had a shower. When I returned, she was brandishing a list of about a dozen names. I knew half of them. They belonged to the acquaintances who had recommended Olivia to me at the start of the winter as this 'wonderful girl' who'd look after my children. The other names on the list, although I didn't know any of them personally, weren't very surprising. It was much the same kind of line-up, with the exception of a shy young man whom she'd got to know at her last job before she'd got the sack, who'd protected her come hell or high water, in the face of all logic – a gracious, sad and silent friend. Apart from this young man, who was studying geography, all or almost all of the others were journalists. All, or almost all, were between fifteen and twenty years older than Olivia. Drawn together by her predicament, they seemed like a guild of godmothers and godfathers. Of presentable godmothers and godfathers, it goes without saying. I knew by then that she'd spare me the trouble of knowing the others.

I wrote telephone numbers next to the names on the list.

'Where do you know all these people from?' I asked as I wrote.

Olivia assumed the bemused expression which suited her so well.

'Haven't I told you about when I came to Paris?'

'I don't think so.'

'Oh well, it was when I came to Paris . . .'

'I thought you went to your sister's.'

'The first time, yes, when I was thirteen. Then I went back to Normandy. I was there for another year before I left for good when I was fourteen. Wait, I'll tell you . . .'

'It's funny, really,' I told my brother that evening on the phone. 'Considering she hates school so much – that's where she met this guy, this singer, I've forgotten his name. Anyway, this guy went round secondary schools putting on performances with the kids. She got involved and was so pleased with the results that she decided to do some promotion for the show. She looked up the addresses of newspapers in the phonebook – and not just any newspapers either: *Le Parisien*, *Libération*, *Le Quotidien* – jumped on the train, and went and saw the journalists on their arts pages. And there you go, that's how she met the people who're coming to dinner here on Tuesday.'

On Tuesday afternoon I did the shopping. I filled a trolley at Franprix and bought a chocolate cake at the bakery. When I got back to the flat,

Olivia wasn't there. I did the cooking and got the table ready. I tidied the living room and laid a fire in the fireplace. Then I drank a cup of tea and waited for the children to come home from school. They arrived, accompanied by Olivia. Their cheeks were pink with cold (cold is the only thing that gives them any colour), and they each had a lollipop stuck in their mouths.

'Happy birthday,' I said to Olivia.

'Hello,' Olivia replied.

'What? What? It's your birthday?' the children protested.

Olivia spent the whole of the rest of the afternoon with them. She didn't offer to lay the table or go and buy bread.

She acted as if nothing was going on.

I told myself that she wasn't used to dinner parties, or birthdays, that she hadn't asked me for anything, that I'd promised I'd do everything. I told myself that she probably wouldn't help with the washing-up afterwards, either. If I wanted to do birthdays, I just had to face up to my responsibilities.

'I remember,' said Étienne Varlat, opening the first bottle of champagne, 'I'd just got back from a story and it was already dark. My secretary whispered in my ear, "There's a young girl waiting for you in your office. She's been here for hours. I told her to come back tomorrow but she said it was very important and that she had plenty of time. She's made herself comfortable and she won't budge." I opened the door of my office and I saw Olivia, sitting on my chair at my desk and leafing through my newspapers. "Hello," she said, "I've been waiting for you."'

Olivia listened to him, laughing, and looking embarrassed as she always did when people talked about her.

'You bet I had all the time in the world, I didn't have anywhere else to go. I would have slept in the street if you hadn't come back . . . So, he turns up, I give him my little story. Then he asks me where I'm going to sleep, I say I don't know. It was nine o'clock already. You should've seen his face!'

'Imagine! This little girl turns up out of the middle of nowhere. I listen nicely to her spiel about deprived kids and then, when I offer to take her home, she says, "Don't worry, I'll manage on my own, thank you very much," and, "Can you tell me when the article's going to come out?"'

The cork slid out smoothly and Étienne poured the first glass.

'I took her back to our house. You stayed a long time, the first time. A month? Two months?'

'Two months,' answered Olivia.

'Oh yes!' said Étienne. 'That was the time you sold my records. Hundreds of records. My whole collection. Ten francs each. God knows who to. "What have you done with my records, Olivia?" I kept asking her. I was hoping she could get them back. But she obviously didn't understand why I was getting so worked up. "I've told you already, I've sold them," she kept saying.'

Olivia grimaced.

'I didn't realize. He had so many records. I thought he'd be pleased I was bringing in some money.'

It was a cheerful dinner. The guests arrived punctually. They had dressed with care. Those with children brought them along. The kids knelt around the low table and silently emptied dishes of almonds and dried fruits.

In Olivia's honour, their parents compared memories which were now almost ten years old and mirrored each other. Olivia camping in their offices, the articles they'd written for her, the times she'd stayed with them. Her habit of suddenly disappearing, so that they couldn't keep track of her, and then returning unexpectedly, either laughing or in tears, trailing turbulence behind her.

I had drunk a fair bit of champagne. I wasn't mixing my drinks and, in that amiable, relaxed mood you get from drinking light wine, I listened to the guests with a warm sensation of fellow-feeling. I was attentive but at one remove. I was tinkering with my mental scales, making them balance. It wasn't that important, in the end, that I loved Olivia. Olivia would always find people to love her. She'd never be alone – that was her strength. When the scales levelled out, when I felt both sides balancing, I was disappointed but also relieved to realize that I wasn't indispensable – or, in fact, even necessary. I was helping Olivia less than she was using me. The champagne finally dissolved a certain image I had of Providence.

As she'd threatened, Olivia disappeared to the other end of the flat, taking the children with her, like a kind of Pied Piper of Hamelin. The rest of us spent the evening discovering our mutual acquaintances. We all worked in a world where the people you meet accumulate; our jobs consumed names and faces.

Olivia and the children had to be called back to bring out the candle-covered cake. I turned out the lights. We'd agreed earlier that Suzanne and Thomas would hold it together, which meant lopsidedly. The wax dripped shakily over the chocolate icing.

Olivia blew out the candles in one go. We all applauded happily. Then we sang 'Happy Birthday' and gave her our presents. I'd bought her a bottle of Chanel No. 5. I've always thought that it's an appropriate scent for a young woman.

At one o'clock, the guests began to climb out of the sofas and gather up their children. They were joyful and slightly tipsy. We said goodbye, promising to see each other again.

After all the guests had gone Olivia picked up her bag and her coat. 'I'm going out,' she said. 'See you. And thanks for the scent.'

She closed the door softly behind her. I stood on the doormat, flabbergasted.

'And what sort of state are you going to be in tomorrow? Eh? What sort of state?' I asked the closed door.

Then, as anticipated, I got down to the washing-up.

19

From the moment I'd kissed Suzanne and Thomas good night and shut their bedroom door, I was reckoning on a quarter of an hour. I grabbed clean clothes from the wardrobe as I walked back down the passage, pushed the bathroom door open with my foot, and turned on the tap. The shower head twisted on the white enamel. I pulled off my sweater and polo shirt in one go and unbuttoned my trousers with one hand while unlacing my shoes with the other. I jumped under the jet of scalding water and was still blinded when I stepped out of the tub. I pulled on the clean clothes, which stuck to my damp skin. I didn't have to choose my shoes, I only had one pair.

I grabbed my keys and said goodbye to Olivia, who was sprawled in front of the telly. I walked briskly to the restaurant, putting my perfume on in the street.

Catching sight of me rushing along the avenue, no one would have thought they'd seen a princess — if anything, I looked like a rough sketch of a girl. Yet I wasn't that far from lonely Cinderella hurrying to the ball in a pumpkin carriage.

I went into the restaurant and sat down at the back of the room. I lit a cigarette.

I waited for Thierry.

I saw him push open the door of the restaurant and my heart turned to mush. Fear and expectation caramelized together to make my eyes shine like boiled sweets.

Usually, we'd sit facing one another and start embarrassed conversations, the hesitant thread of which we'd immediately lose. As a talker, I found this shyness unbearable; it made me feel like some stilted, stuck-up young woman. But then we'd go to bed, at his place, at mine or in a hotel. And there you have it. I adored, I adored, I adored sleeping with him.

I wasn't the only one, admittedly. But I couldn't blame myself for that. All the energy he didn't put into his work he devoted to making himself loved. He'd become very accomplished at it and the men who knew him envied him, with good reason. As for women, they'd stare at him, amused and curious. They suspected that he contained an ocean of delights. To those who would swim, he was offering his pedalo.

So many love affairs should have made a man happy. But there was nothing happy about Thierry. He was sad, often he was even sinister. He cried in his sleep, his face buried in the pillow – I'd try, unsuccessfully, to wake him up. In despair, he was irresistible.

Poor Thierry, so much seduction had completely ruined love for him. He felt he was badly loved, and he was right. He thought he couldn't love anyone, and he was wrong. He turned the world into an asylum where he was the head lunatic. He didn't know what he wanted, unlike all those women who knew exactly what they wanted: him.

In the end he'd get in a rage and turn it against himself. Damaged and disappointed, he'd wind up in the bed of a new woman. And it would start all over again.

✻

I had entered the dance with enthusiasm. To summarize: I loved him, although perhaps I didn't, he didn't love me, although perhaps he did, I was unhappy, he wasn't happy, we never stopped splitting up, but separated or together we weren't in bed together any less frequently and very happy we were to be there, too, side by side, sinking into sleep with contented smiles on our faces. The mornings, however, were often difficult.

Given the circumstances it was pretty ridiculous to talk about love.

'I think it's chemical,' I'd say, my face against his neck. 'I think it's olfactory. I'm chained to you by my nose.'

And I'd breathe in childhood smells which made me want to burst into tears.

'Get rid of him,' Cécile would say, disgustedly.

I'd be pitiful and tearful. I'd agree. I'd fail to get rid of him.

'He's dead good-looking,' Olivia would say. She bumped into him sometimes in the morning as he fled, his coat flapping open. He wasn't that keen on saying hello to my children when they woke up. 'He's got a lovely smile.'

My brother, who knew him well, didn't say anything.

We broke up, yet again, at the end of a disastrous weekend. It was almost dark and we were walking down the street together. It was nearly time for me to go home to the flat; on Sunday evenings Jean-Patrick brought the children back at seven.

'I'd like you to tell me something,' I said, gripped by sentimental delusions, forgetting the chemical nature of the universe.

I waited in vain for a response. He carried on walking beside me, looking preoccupied and discontented.

'A little thing,' I insisted desperately, mired in an idealistic conception of the relations between human beings.

He stopped and looked at me unkindly.

'If you want to know if I love you,' he said, articulating each syllable clearly, 'you know already, no, I don't love you.'

The words felt like the blows of a piston. My eyes filled with tears,
which spilled over and began to roll down my face.

'Oooh,' I said.

'And not only that,' he added, keen to exhaust the subject, 'but I don't
want to live with you either. Ever.'

'Oooh,' I answered and my tears were accompanied with loud,
unlovely hiccups.

Oddly enough, he didn't walk off when he'd finished his declaration.
He stayed at my side, marching through the damp, cold night. I didn't
try to run away either, which any wounded weasel would have done if
it had been in my place, instinctively aware of the folly of going for a
stroll with a poacher.

We cut a fine figure, tramping through Paris at a resolute pace, me
sniffling and wiping my eyes with the back of my sleeve, Thierry
keeping his hands soberly in his pockets.

Still weeping like the Zambezi, my sight blurred, I caught sight of
the time on a public clock.

'Oh no,' I said, wringing my hands, 'the kids will be on their way
back and I'm late. You've got to give me your phone card, and wait for
me.'

I dived into a telephone box. Thierry stood outside the glass door,
stamping his feet.

Thomas answered.

'Dad had to leave, he had some friends coming round. But he said
he'd call us when he got back to make sure you were home . . .'

'I'm coming. Don't let anybody in while you're waiting.'

We hurled ourselves into the nearest Metro station. I ignored the
compassionate looks of the other passengers in the carriage.

Thierry left me at the foot of my block.

'So long,' he said and walked away.

At the door of the flat, I wiped my face and took a deep breath. I hung a forced smile under my sentimental nose. Then I turned the key in the lock.

'Hi, guys,' I called, taking off my wet jacket. 'Not too hungry, are we?'

I went into the kitchen and opened the fridge.

'Hey, mum,' Suzanne said behind me, 'shall I read you my poetry?'

'Go on,' I said, taking a packet of butter, and Suzanne declaimed,

> *My hands are black*
> *and the countryside is grey,*
> *the wind blows and*
> *I see the light of the sky*
> *which makes my life sparkle*
> *since I was li . . .*

In the pan, the butter was a white, foaming pool. I broke the eggs.

As soon as the children were in bed, I called Thierry.

'Yes?' a glum voice answered.

'It's me,' I said, as if we were having a polite chit-chat. 'I wanted to tell you that I got back OK and that I'm feeling better now. How about you, are you alright?'

'Not great,' the voice said. 'I've taken some stuff, I think I'm ill. I'm going to hang up, sorry.'

'Go ahead,' I said. 'I'll call back in a quarter of an hour to see if everything's alright.'

The moment I put the receiver down, I remembered an affair I'd had with a man a long time before. He too sometimes took drugs in the evening, and then he'd have to cut our telephone conversations short. He was indecisive, and married to a very pretty woman. All of us had suffered a lot and the affair had ended miserably.

The memory of it was like being slapped a second time. I don't believe that handsome princes rouse sleeping princesses with a kiss – how could they, kisses put you to sleep. Slaps are what wake you up. I'd suddenly had enough of sad stories and vulgar love affairs.

When I called back a quarter of an hour later, Thierry wasn't ill any more, just out of it. I was reassured: you never know.

'Things are fine,' he said, slightly groggy.

'Bye,' I said. 'Goodnight.'

I felt calm then, free to leave him to himself and to return to myself. Sitting beside the telephone, I felt broken-down with tiredness. You can't count on people who keep relapsing, you can't help them, you can't love them. They discourage love.

Before I went to bed, I played back the answering machine. The last message was practically inaudible. I had to listen to it twice before I realized that it was the photographer I was meant to be working with the following day. He asked me to call him back, but I didn't.

I fell asleep with a pleasurable feeling of bathing in my body, a body which felt the right size for me, neither too baggy nor too tight. I was free, but I didn't feel that proud. On that victorious evening, I was General Custer. All my good loves were dead loves.

SECOND PART

I

It's the middle of December. Our family unit has attained a kind of serenity. On weekdays we have supper at about eight. We generally get up at seven thirty.

I've done a swap for Thierry and his carnival of spellbinding sorrows. I've taken to my still-warm bed the photographer I met the following day. His name is Denis.

Olivia isn't taking drugs, at least not to my knowledge, which amounts to abstinence. She isn't stuffing herself, either. Alcohol is our sedative, our mind-altering drug. There's nothing festive about our routine drinking. I can't see much difference between a bottle of booze and a packet of Lysanxia.

Both of us could be taken for more or less normal people.

Olivia is trailing round the flat in her pyjamas, drinking coffee. She follows me into my room and watches me make the bed.

'Is he nice, Denis?' she asks, looking doubtful – although she could be looking sleepy, it's hard to tell in the morning.

'Very nice,' I say, smoothing out the mattress with the flat of my hand. 'Nice and not a pain and I think he's good-looking, don't you?'

She agrees with me, pretty good-looking, yes. By the way, have I heard from Thierry?

'No,' I say proudly, 'it's over.'

'Hmm,' Olivia says, 'pity, I liked his smile. Still, never mind, the important thing is that you're happy. You're happy, at least?'

'Very happy.'

And it's true.

Looking back, I realize that confessions emerge like icebergs. At first you see the tip poking out of the water. You say to yourself: Oh look, a little piece of ice, I'll steer clear of that. You think you're steering clear of it, but actually you're still right next to it. While you're shilly-shallying, the iceberg keeps on rising. You haven't seen anything coming but suddenly there it is, rolling in the water, massive and mountainous, giving you vertigo, blocking off the horizon. I had come across the frozen tip of the iceberg several times, but I'd always stoutly managed to ignore it. I think mid-December was the start of the time that ended up with me smashing headfirst into the ice, as I tried to look the other way.

*

Olivia sits at my desk, gripping the handle of her cup firmly. She rests the slice of bread she's eating on her knees. Rain is lashing against the windowpanes.

'At first,' she says, 'I couldn't get to sleep when you were with a guy.'

I lift the duvet up with a sweeping movement of my arms. It floats above the bed and then falls back down with a soft noise. I give the edges a tug. Then I grab a pillow.

'I'd be waiting for you to ask me to join you in bed.'

I pause for a fraction of a second, the pillow hesitating above my head. She adds, 'It always ended up like that before. In bed.'

With sex, Olivia adopts different tactics from those that worked for her with drugs. Rather than heroic detoxification and brutal revelations, she prefers gradual exposure, which suits me. If I'd had to choose, knowing what I was going to hear, I'd have done the same as her. I, too, would have proceeded by stages.

My break-up with Thierry paved the way. She knows how upset I can get. More than once, sitting opposite her in the evening, I've lost it and started to cry. She's never tried to run away. 'Come on, it's not that bad, it's the same for me too. Here, have a drink, all these stories make me sick,' she'd say.

And she'd stay with me until I'd calmed down. She'd only leave once she'd seen me talking and smiling; then she'd go upstairs. I'd curl up in a ball in my bed, knowing her maid's room was overhead. I'd close my eyes and listen to her footsteps and I'd bank on everything being there in the morning: her, her ciggies and her coffee.

And in the morning, to my amazement, she'd be there. 'Here you go,' she'd say, thrusting a boiling cup of coffee at me, 'don't burn yourself, I've never known anyone who works as hard as you do, I think you're incredible, don't spill it, you could be twenty, sit up slowly or you'll spill it.'

More than once Olivia has bailed out my sorrow with a coffee cup, bending at the waist over the edge of our little boat.

I'd open my eyes, looking a hundred years old and hungover. 'Thanks,' I'd mumble.

'It's nothing,' Olivia would say in a ringing voice, 'anyone would do the same.' And she'd exhale a great plume of white smoke through her nostrils.

'Over.'

At her request, I'm repeating to Olivia that it's over. She has an admiring look on her face.

'Still, it would be true to say you still love him,' she says in a satis-fied voice.

'Love? What does love mean when you're as miserable as sin?'

I blow my own trumpet. I flaunt the wisdom I've acquired over the last sixty-eight hours.

'Still, you've got to be tough to send a guy on his way, that's really strong.'

She rubs her hands. I take a breath, feeling the air and blood enter-ing my lungs. I know I seem unshakeable to her. But how would I ever have survived my chaos without her?

'Me,' she says, 'I can't do it.'

'What?'

'Chuck someone. Even if he's a bastard, I can't throw him out, he has to chuck me first. Even if a guy does things to me that you wouldn't do to an animal, I just end up giving him a pat on the back. I can't get angry.'

I shake the duvet. I think about what Olivia's just told me. I thump my bed hard. The idea of inviting Olivia into it disgusts me. I'm very fond of her but I prefer everybody to keep their bodies to themselves. Later in the morning, when I switch on my computer, I say out loud to myself, 'People are mad.'

Olivia is doing her own thing in the corner. She replies politely, 'You said it.'

As the menu comes up on the screen I don't think people are mad. I think that if people were cannibals, those men would have eaten her. They don't love her the way you love a plant which you water and keep in the light, admiring its leaves and its goodness, looking forward to its flowers and fruits. No. They love her the way you love a piece of meat that has to be eaten quickly before it rots. They kill her and eat her while her blood is still warm and her soft breath is still within her body.

I click on 'Office', I open 'Misc', I call up 'Annual Report', I light a cigarette.

Two days later, in the lobby of the agency, I bump into Étienne Varlat. I hardly know him, but I've seen him around a lot. He's tall, thin and warm-hearted, and I was glad when he came to Olivia's birthday dinner.

'What are you doing here?' he says.

'Same as you, freelance work.'

He draws himself up to his full height and replies guardedly.

'This is rare for me. It's just because I need the money. I'm a journalist, I don't do propaganda.'

I'm not offended. None of the freelances I know respect their work, but we all need money. Cynicism is invariably what keeps us going. Étienne and I head for the nearest café and I listen to him explaining himself.

Over our beers, we soon get round to talking about Olivia and our affection for her.

'What I find staggering,' says Étienne, 'is her ability to laugh about everything. I remember one afternoon when she turned up in my office. She was completely hysterical. "Hey Étienne," – she was giggling uncontrollably, almost crying with laughter – "Étienne, guess what's just happened to me?" Her laughter was contagious and I started laughing too. "Go on, how am I supposed to guess," ". . . guess what, I've just been raped again." She laughed for a few more seconds, then she passed out. I took her to hospital. I stayed at her bedside while the doctors examined her. She was in a terrible state. I held her hand, she didn't say anything but, when she looked at me, she smiled. She tried really hard to laugh some more. She was shaking her head.'

2

That evening we play Monopoly. Suzanne is cheating, without malice. Thomas is getting infuriated. I'm bored, I throw the dice too hard and they skid across the table and fall onto the floor. Olivia is the only one interested in the game. She's the banker, she tells the children off, she dives to pick up the dice. She ponders whether she should buy rue de la Paix. She wrinkles her nose. I watch her. She makes me laugh.

When the children are in bed, I tell her about my conversation with Étienne Varlat.

'Oh yeah,' she says, 'poor Étienne, he couldn't get over it, I was standing in his office, shaking – I had burns all over my body, they'd burnt me too – and the only thing I could do was crack up with laughter. You should have seen Étienne's face, even you would have laughed. Anyway, the main thing is that he took me to the hospital. He was really kind, I can't tell you how kind he was. I've still got burn marks on my breasts.'

I refuse to think that the person I'm talking to has scars from burns on her breasts.

'Did you bring charges?'

She looks at me, aghast.

'For a rape?'

'Olivia.' My voice is very calm. I am just beginning to comprehend how differently we experience the social order. 'Olivia,' I say, with a gravity that sounds somehow affected, 'burning is a barbaric act, rape is a crime.'

'Yes,' Olivia agrees amiably, 'so?'

'So, men who do that go to court, they get fifteen or twenty years in prison. That's the law.'

She shrugs.

'Oh really, so you expect someone who's been raped repeatedly to go and tell the police, do you? Sorry to disturb you Mister Policeman but this time I've really had enough . . . not to mention all the stuff that was going on with drugs. When someone's in the shit, they don't go and mess about with the police, they keep their mouth shut.'

'But Olivia,' I say weakly, 'if they're a minor, the law's meant to protect them.'

'It protects people like you. Not the rest of us, trust me. I'd have been dumped in a juvenile court, then the judge would have stuck me in a hostel or maybe even prison, and you've got no idea what it's like in there.'

'But didn't you have a social worker, someone from social services, someone to stand up for you?'

Olivia titters.

'Yes, there was one woman. Poor thing, she threw me out in the end. I was unbearable. She ended up saying to me, "I don't give a damn about what happens to you: since you don't want to listen to anything anyone tells you, you can sort it out on your own." And that was it, I was struck off the list. I could take it easy.'

She has an intrepid expression on her face and a defiant look in her eyes. She thinks it's fair enough; if you fool around, you've got to be prepared for trouble. You have to pay for your mistakes. You don't have to be Einstein to figure that out.

She has no conception of the law as something which listens to people, weighs their faults and allots their punishment. She believes in an order which rewards the strong and grinds the weak to a pulp. She's pig-ignorant; all she knows is the law of gangsters.

I listen carefully, like a parish priest, and reply with carefully chosen words. I insist on seeing her as a victim, halfwit that I am. Then I begin to rave, but she doesn't understand a word of what I say. She's convinced she's guilty. Her world is divided into two castes: winners at the top, guilty at the bottom. She's only got a slim chance of clawing her way up amongst the winners, so she thinks she can be crafty and cheat and lie as much as she likes: when the time comes for settling up, she's going to be for it anyway.

I don't know how to get her to understand that she's a victim. I abandon my prejudices. I appeal to the law, draping myself in the glory of the Republic.

'Right,' I fling back, 'that's as may be, but the law exists to punish crimes. It's designed for everybody, including you.'

Wasted effort. I am all alone in my toga. Olivia doesn't give a toss about the regalia of the Republic.

'Yeah, so you say,' she retorts, insolently.

'That's right, I do say! You could even bring charges now! I think you can take someone to court ten years after the crime.'

She brushes me aside self-importantly with the back of her hand.

'If I press charges for every time it's happened to me, then the police aren't going to have time for anything else. It doesn't matter, it's in the past. Forget it.'

She tidies away the Monopoly. She carefully piles up the orange and purple notes, stacks the houses and hotels in the box, and forces the lid shut.

The floodgates have been opened. The allusions she's scattered through our conversations in the last few weeks have become a torrent. She seems stronger for it, she's losing weight at a rate of knots and she's become very pretty again. She hums to herself. She falls ill with every conceivable ailment.

She trawls the surgeries with her healthcare card. She offers doctors her blind faith and then swiftly withdraws it in a series of abrupt counter-offensives. She brings home frantic diagnoses which we then submit to long, contradictory analysis.

'Abscesses,' she says decisively, 'that's cocaine. What does that dentist know about it, stupid idiot?'

She treats herself half-heartedly, her gums swell up and we have to call emergency dentists in the middle of the night.

She stuffs herself with Prozac.

'It's pure hell without any pills,' she says, contemplating the oblong tablet dolefully. 'I might as well take them.'

And then *whoops*, she downs the tablet in one.

'I can't stop, or I'll have a really bad comedown. I tell you, this all comes from my mother. She was too delicate. I've inherited her genes.'

She often has stomach pains, and suffers from dizzy spells.

'Could it be an ulcer?' I wonder.

'No way, you've obviously never had one. I reckon it's to do with my vagina. Sometimes I wonder if it could be from what happened to me when I was a kid, those little sticks that old man put in me, maybe I got an infection and I didn't get it treated and that's why I'm having discharges now. Smart, huh? What do you think?'

I make a face as I turn it over in my mind. When I think about it, yes, little sticks; wood's not that clean, without an antiseptic there could be a risk of infection.

'What does the gynaecologist say?'

'He says antibiotics. He wants me to take them for the rest of my life, antibiotics and stuff like that. I'm going to chuck the packet away. Would you trust a gynaecologist who said that, eh?'

She chucks the packet away.

We take the lift together. I'm leaving for work, she's going out to buy bread. Outside there's a bright wintry light and a marvellous liquid blue sunshine. We walk down to the corner of the street. 'By the way,' Olivia says as we sit down side by side on a bench, facing the erratic morning tide of cars on the avenue. The biting air gives her rosy-apple cheeks. It turns my nose red.

'By the way,' Olivia asks, 'are you OK?'

She leans an elbow on the back of the bench and turns towards me, smiling. I don't know anyone apart from her who's still sincerely interested in the answer to this question. Even I've given up on it.

I grimace in endorsement and nod my head. 'Yes, yes, yes, I'm OK.'

'The children are OK as well, don't you think?'

Yes, they seem well. 'It's thanks to you if everything's OK, them, me, the flat, you know.'

'Maybe. I'm glad you're feeling better. You're not as depressed as you were, now, are you?'

'No, not as much as I was, there's no reason to be. I did the right thing getting rid of Thierry.'

It's her turn to nod thoughtfully. I look at her. Her eyes are shining, maybe it's the cold or maybe she's also crying a little bit. I don't know.

'Oh fuck,' she says, rubbing her face with her open hands, 'I wish I was OK as well, I'm so weak. Sometimes I think I'm better, but I can't seem to make it last, I keep slipping back.'

She wipes her eyes with the back of her hand. I look at the time on the watches in the window of a jewellery shop. I stand up and adjust my backpack.

'Sorry, I've got to go, but listen to me, I don't know anyone in the world who's as brave and strong as you are. I've got to run, I'm going to be late.'

Unthinkingly, I give her hair a friendly stroke. She shudders and hunches her shoulders abruptly. I say again, 'Sorry, I forgot.'

'See you later, princess,' I call over my shoulder. I run to the Metro.

3

Olivia is talking but I can't hear what she's saying. I look like I'm listening but actually I'm deaf, the words don't reach my memory, they slide off and disappear. It's probably because I can't listen to everything she says.

I'm beginning to have doubts, too, about the reality of her words. I couldn't swear that she really told me some old man put little sticks in her vagina. Perhaps I've made it up. I'm worn out by these shards of confession that constantly embed themselves in our conversations.

I brush away the crumbs on the table with the back of my sleeve.

'I don't understand. Explain it to me again, clearly. What was this fucking shambles at the Lerouillys'?'

Olivia folds her arms with a diligent air.

'It wasn't really the Lerouillys,' she corrects me. 'It was the neighbours. They'd come and pick me up from the farm and take me to the woods. When it was over, the little business, they'd give me some sweets and they'd take me home. You know what children are like, they think a packet of sweets is brilliant, it's enough for them.'

'And Madame Lerouilly? She let you go off walking in the woods with all the old men of the neighbourhood? She saw you coming home with sweeties and she didn't say anything?'

'It's the country, people have got their own way of thinking. I don't know what she thought. She was already old then, she couldn't keep an eye on everything. She'd got too much going on at home as it was – her daughter, two grandsons and the other four from social services.'

'But didn't you say anything to her?'

'Me? What was I supposed to say to her? I took the sweets. I wasn't dead. I thought I'd been naughty. I didn't feel like getting a beating from Monsieur Lerouilly.'

Olivia tells me that she also went to catechism while all this was going on and took her first communion at Sunday mass. She still liked school and she was a good pupil. No, she wasn't especially unhappy. She wasn't mad about Mme Lerouilly either, she smiles, but then I must remember that she'd never known her mother, she'd only ever had Mme Lerouilly, and she's got nothing against the woman. What should she have against her, anyway?

I ask her what's become of the other kids who were placed with the Lerouilly family. Yes, she hears about them, now and again. The twins are in prison, that was predictable. The girl's probably dead now – last time Olivia heard about her she was in a real mess, heroin, AIDS. The Lerouilly children are studying. The sons are farmers, the daughter's a civil servant. Yes, she's seen them since, occasionally.

'Any other questions?'

'No,' I say, 'that's fine. I like to know who they are, the people you talk about.'

I have a clearer picture now and in a way it's reassuring: the farm, the church, the school, the wood, the sweeties. I don't ask for details about the walks, I'm not crazy. Before I close proceedings, I inquire, 'And old man Lerouilly and his sons, what about them?'

Olivia doesn't answer. She goes and puts on a record. She won't say any more about it. I'll have to make do with shards. Later, when we are talking about something completely different, she tells me that at night she fenced off her bed with string, hoping that that would stop them coming and feeling her up while she slept.

But right now I don't want to know anything else about that period. I don't want to know who felt her up – the twins, the sons or the father. I've got enough of a picture of the devastation, I have no use for further pain.

Olivia makes the most of her latest confession straight away.

'I'm going away for the weekend,' she announces joyfully.

I'm at the sink, washing up.

'Great. Where to?'

'Normandy.'

I turn off the tap and wipe my hands.

'What on earth are you going to do in Normandy?'

She gives me a broad smile.

'I'm going to see Madame Lerouilly.'

'What?'

'She sent me a little letter for my birthday. Here, have a look.'

She hands me a yellowish envelope. I take out a hideous card and read, *Happy Birthday, little one.* Signed: *Madame Lerouilly.* The biro has leaked, the writing is cretinous.

Olivia senses that I'm touched and becomes emotional.

'I always make sure that she's got an address. She sends me a card every birthday.'

She takes the envelope back, folds it carefully and tucks it into the pocket of her jeans. I want to smash everything.

'It's not that difficult to send a card. I'll send you a hundred, tomorrow if you like.'

I've hit a raw nerve. Olivia hangs her head. Shit, I could slap myself – in fact, I do, with the flat of my still soapy hand. 'No, wait. I didn't mean that. I think it's very nice that she writes to you. So she still sends you cards after all these years, does she?'

'Yes,' murmurs Olivia.

'That shows how fond she is of you. You really have to care about somebody to write to them every birthday. What about old man Lerouilly? Is he dead?'

'No,' Olivia says, 'but I'm not going there to see him, you've no idea what a tyrant he is. Even the priest's afraid of him. Like I said, I'm just going to see Madame Lerouilly. I'll arrive there in the morning, she'll come out into the yard and bring me a cup of coffee, and we'll have a chat without the father knowing. Then I'll go for a little walk and I'll come back in the evening.'

'That's nice,' I say.

It breaks my heart. I know it's not nice. That old whore is family to her, that wretched farm a leafy paradise, and the whole thing represents forgiveness for those childhood trysts. But I can't say anything. What she's going to look for in that godforsaken hole is not unfamiliar to me.

It's the brightly coloured scraps of childhood. And all the anger in the world can't give her another childhood. So I don't throw Mme Lerouilly out with the bathwater. 'That poor woman. She'll be so happy to see you,' I say unctuously. Olivia is consoled and insists on showing me her train tickets. I look at them, I turn them over, I admire them.

She doesn't have a single photo from the Lerouilly years. What did they buy with the money from social services, I wonder. Land, fertilizer, worms. Most likely they stuck it in a chicory jar. One thing's for sure – they saved themselves the price of an Instamatic and I've ended up poring over some train tickets.

4

I travel a lot. Well, I make frequent small trips. Since I started this job, I've visited most French towns several times, big and small. I've been to Aubagne, to Grenoble, to Nancy, Bourg-en-Bresse and Le Puy, to Biarritz and Saint-Quentin, to Reims, Amiens, Ajaccio and Le Mans, to La Mure and Brest, to Toulouse, Colmat and Chartres, to Lille, to Lorient, to Lyons. I've met miners, insurance agents, farmers, teachers, electricians, bankers, researchers, computer scientists, welders, postmen – all sorts of people, basically.

They talk to me about their professions, that's what I'm paid for. They all end up saying at least one interesting thing, sometimes it's a very small thing. I store it away in my mind and forget where I've stored it. I remember the tone of a voice, a mountain road, a face, a milk-white sky.

I've made up for my primary school years. If someone asked me – God how I wish somebody would – I could now draw a map of France, freehand. I know the names of the rivers and the massifs, of the regions and airports, I know what secondhand goods people deal in, what they live off and what they lack, I can describe their houses and the steeples of their churches. I've become good at geography twenty-five years too late. If only I could go back and start again, I wouldn't lose my crayons, I'd know how to go about things so much better – in geography and everything else. I was too young for too long, I was constantly making mistakes. I'd get lost in the street. How I regret having been left alone with my youth, how I regret not having been born older. I wouldn't have cried so much. Everything is so much simpler when you know the rules of the game in advance. I'm not just talking about love. I'm talking about geography as well.

I leave the flat very early in the morning to catch a train or a plane. I leave without a sound, pulling the door closed behind me without remorse. Olivia will organize getting up. I'm not indispensable to breakfast. On the other hand, I make sure that I'm back by suppertime. At out first meeting Olivia warned me, 'I can't cook.'

'No problem. I can,' I said.

So I come home.

It's late afternoon, I'm in Nevers, and I'm freezing. This time I'm not going to make it. The ice is so heavy on the cables and has covered the rails so thoroughly that the trains will be late, 'an unforeseeable delay,' the loudspeaker crackles, 'one or two hours.' I call from a phone box and tell Olivia; all she has to do is root around in the fridge, she can rustle something up, it's not that hard, don't wait for me, I'm on my way home. I hang around on the concourse and buy myself a can of beer and a Toblerone. I sit on the train with my feet up and my knees wedged against the back of the seat in front. I fall asleep and dream I'm sleeping with a boy whose face keeps changing, which isn't restful at all.

*

I get a taxi home from the station. The driver is African. He gives me the addresses of two restaurants which serve elephant. I thank him, take my notebook out of my bag and write the addresses down but I know I'm never going to go. Elephant, what an idea. Why not gorilla? Must we always fricassee our relatives and fellow creatures? Often I have doubts. I no longer know where to draw the line between compassion and stupidity.

I take the lift. I'm happy to come home this evening, just as I was happy to leave this morning. I take the key out of my pocket and open the door. It's bitterly cold in the flat, and what's this rancid smoke hanging in the passage? Who's been burning tyres?

I shrug the bag off my shoulder and go into the kitchen, Olivia's at the stove, red-faced, her hair a complete mess. She looks at me, sorrowfully.

'Evening. I did what you said.'

She's shaking a pan of bubbling oil with little spasmodic jerks.

'Watch out, you'll burn yourself.'

Immersed in the oil are three chalky white lumps covered in sooty marks. The objects are intact despite the violent heat, jumping around but refusing to fall apart. I can't imagine how they've remained so rigid, and then I realize. They're still frozen. Four blocks of frozen matter hurled into boiling oil. This strikes me as an act of almost medieval brutality.

Now I know why the kitchen windows are wide open. The flat's minus five, maximum. A ferocious draught rushes through the stellar cold, I bet the living-room windows are open too.

'What is it?'

I indicate the oil with a discreet movement of my chin and speak in a low voice. I don't want to antagonize Olivia, she seems tense enough already.

'Chicken. Can't you tell?'

'Was there some chicken?'

'Well yeah, I got it out of the freezer.'

'You could have made some eggs, I bought them yesterday . . .'

'I asked the children: eggs or chicken? They said chicken, so I'm doing chicken. Of course I don't know how to make it, but you knew that, didn't you?'

Olivia abandons her cooking. I don't stop to answer her or even to take off my coat. I run to the cooker, grab the handle of the pan and tip it into the sink, dumping the oil and the sad bits of chicken. They make a whimpering noise as they fall. The oil congeals and forms arabesques on the white enamel.

'Frozen food's tricky,' I mumble, 'if you've never done it, it's easy to make mistakes, it happens to everybody. I was the same the first time . . .'

I'm talking to myself. Olivia's left the kitchen.

'Pizza's best,' she observes as I burst into the living room a minute later to shut the windows which are letting in a strong, frosty wind.

Thomas is sitting in front of the TV wrapped in his duvet. He stares at the screen with the tip of his nose peeking out of the cover. Beneath his snowy forehead, his red, twinkling nose looks like a ruby. I turn off the TV.

'Where's Suzanne?'

'In her room,' whispers Thomas. 'She was cold.'

'Well, she can stay there for now. I'm going to turn on the heating and cook some eggs.'

'Because you can get pizzas delivered,' Olivia continues, her arms hanging by her sides, a vindictive look on her face. 'It doesn't cost that much. And it's much easier.'

I sense the reproach, but I don't know the cause. My stinginess? My mood swings?

'OK, fine. I'll put two hundred in an envelope on the bookshelf next time. Then all you'll have to do is order your bloody pizzas.'

'Oh, mum,' Thomas says, standing up in his duvet, 'why're you getting in such a strop? We were doing fine before you came and now it's all a disaster. You should come home later if you just want to ruin everything. We'd have managed to have supper alright without you.'

I keep quiet. He is right. I should have hung about in town and not come straight back home to be scolded in minus ten in an atmosphere thick with the oily fumes of frozen chicken. But now it's Olivia's turn to be indignant. She raises her arms to heaven in outrage, reversing her allegiances.

'Hey you! That's your mother you're talking to! She's out all day at work, earning money for us! Is that all you can say to her when she gets home? That she shouldn't bother coming back? Do you think she likes that?'

Betrayed, Thomas lies low under his duvet. He thought he was defending shared interests, but he'd forgotten an essential fact: Olivia, above all, is a legitimist. He goes off silently to ask Suzanne for asylum.

Ten minutes later we're sitting at the table with eggs and pasta in front of us. I'm not very hungry and the children are picking at their food. They're tired, and I know they'd have preferred chicken, though they don't dare say so. They go to bed without pudding. Olivia cleans her plate with a bit of bread. 'Did you forget I told you I don't know how to cook?' she asks plaintively.

I hate her when she bores me senseless with her pathetic excuses, I hate her when she acts dumb, I hate her when she takes me for a total idiot.

'Stop whining, everyone knows how to cook, you just have to have a go. There's nothing to it, I'll teach you. It's just common sense, with pasta, say, and a tin of tuna . . .'

But she shakes her head sadly, and interrupts.

'You don't understand. I don't care, cooking doesn't interest me. Forget it.'

5

Olivia gets up early in the morning, she has to go to the doctor. She's found a good vascular specialist.

'Got to watch out. Did you know that your legs can kill you?'

I didn't know. I'd never suspected the legs specifically, but I'm not really surprised. What can't kill you? Toes?

'And are you seeing a psychiatrist?'

'You mean a psychotherapist?'

Olivia smiles knowingly. As it happens, she's just found one. I still marvel that this girl who's unaware of the existence of Marx is so well informed about that of Freud.

Her interest dates from the time of her first committal to Sainte Anne and the conversations she had with the head of the department, whom she often talks about, never mentioning his name without his title, 'Doctor Cajoudiara'. Dr Cajoudiara enjoyed talking to her, and even wrote to her from time to time. On several occasions, he asked her to come back and see him. He warned her about crack. He was the sort of person who liked a joke, and Olivia made him laugh. She knows where he practises now: he went home to Guadeloupe and she got a letter from him there.

I like it when his musical name comes up. Cajoudiara. I imagine him sitting behind his desk in a white coat, wryly surveying a half-crazy fifteen-year-old and trying to show her enough love and intelligence to get her through to adulthood.

Stories about Dr Cajoudiara always mark a good phase, a respite from bad memories, an awakening from the nightmare. Olivia and I dissect his advice meticulously. We speculate, we feel edified. Through the mediation of Dr Cajoudiara we open up paths and plant avenues of trees that will live a hundred years.

'What's the new doctor called?'

'Hang on, I'm trying to remember. Damn, I've forgotten his name . . . It's funny you should ask me that today, because I had my first session yesterday.'

'And?'

'You should see his eyes . . .'

'No, I mean: And, what did you say to him?'

'Nothing, really.'

By asking indiscreet questions, I find out that she doesn't tell this new psychotherapist anything. She doesn't dare. When she does force herself to talk to him, she lies. She omits, she ignores, she tampers with the truth. Not a word about the delights of drugs, not a word about the quagmire of her childhood.

'And did you lie to Cajoudiara as well?'

'Oh no, Cajoudiara wasn't the same. He'd seen others like me. He knew about the street, about drugs. He knew what it's like when everything's hectic. This one, Beautiful Eyes, he's never seen anything. He's all fresh and neat behind his desk. I'd never dare.'

'And discussing it with a man, it's too much for me,' she adds with a gentle laugh.

'So what good does it do?'

She becomes serious again.

'I don't know, do I? I'm waiting to see. Do you always know what the point is of everything you say to all the people you meet?'

Thrilled with her Saturday in Normandy, Olivia spends the next weekend at her sister and brother-in-law's. She often talks about her nephew and niece. She doesn't trust her sister and she's full of motherly concern and anxiety for the children. Her sister and brother-in-law have too much money. She's worried about bad schools, delinquency, bulimia. She says that the children are like her, Olivia. When she starts talking about genes, I realize she's worrying herself sick.

When she comes back on Sunday evening, there is a list of confused complaints. The nephew smokes dope. The brother-in-law has done four years in prison. The children are being brought up badly.

The iceberg looms dangerously. I steer clear of it.

When I come back from work, I find Denis sitting in the hall, on the bottom step of the staircase, waiting for me. I take him by the hand and pull him unceremoniously to his feet. Mme Alvez's beautiful eyes are never far from the window of her flat and I value their respect. He's brought two little cameras with him, which he wants to give to Thomas and Suzanne.

'You don't mind if I meet your children, do you?'

I tell him, brutally, that it's fine: Thomas and Suzanne are used to visitors. We're always entertaining, we like new faces. He needn't think he's too special, he's just a welcome guest. He can have supper with us if he wants. Denis declines the invitation, he's busy.

The children bend over backwards to put him at his ease. Suzanne performs her latest piece of choreography. Thomas teaches him a trick with matches. Never mind that neither of them has ever taken a photo, they both admire the little cameras while they eat the bowls of peanuts. I watch them with tender pride, they're courteous and very sensitive to people.

I serve vodka in the glasses that the mustard comes in. To my amazement, Olivia hardly says a word. She smiles with her head tipped to one side and looks at Denis with the eyes of an adoring schoolgirl. I feel out of my depth, realizing that I don't recognize her in this mood. Elbows on the table, she simpers.

I don't like this fake expression, it's not her, she's so much prettier, for God's sake. I get up and put on a record. Suzanne twirls round the room in a rapture, bumps into the mantelpiece and decides to give up and write a poem instead. Thomas, probably deciding that he's given enough to this man who quite possibly won't last, lies flat on his stomach on the sofa and reads the phonebook. We adults chat and I crumple the empty peanut bag in my hand. Olivia conducts an astonishing ocular ballet around Denis, lowering her eyes, raising them again, avoiding his eyes and then staring straight into them without blinking. She keeps laughing for no reason at all or at the wrong moment, with her hand clasped over her mouth. I have a lump in my throat. I don't offer anyone any more vodka, I put the bottle away; I don't search out any fresh peanuts, I throw the empty packet in the bin.

Denis leaves, planting an anodyne kiss on my cheek. He promises me in a whisper that he'll come back later, in the night.

'If you like.'

I answer curtly. I can't be all things at once. There's a time and a place for everything. The time for whispers comes before or after but never between six and nine o'clock on a weekday evening. I'm sure I've already told him that. He could at least try and adapt.

Thomas shuts the door behind him.

'He wouldn't be a little bit in love with you, that man, would he?' he asks, kicking the doormat out of the way.

I avoid answering. Thomas gets back on the sofa.

As I cook, I whistle merrily and think of Denis. People should end affairs more often. Heaven, it seems, likes separations; it opens doors to those who close them. I raise my eyes to the ceiling where the angels are watching and offer up my thanks.

Denis came into my life the very next day after I split up with Thierry. We'd spent the day working together; then, in the evening, as the plane started its descent over Paris, we shared a whisky, and a kiss. A few days later we continued the exchange in bed. We saw each other again. The ten years between us are a godsend. They neutralize any resentments or competition. We feel nothing but curiosity and the desire to help each other. All this won't last, it's an enchantment.

He comes to see me in the middle of the night, because he works late and likes to go out afterwards. He phones and sometimes he wakes me up. I make a cup of tea while I wait for him, then he scratches on the door and there he is. What a wonderful companion, joyful, articulate and attentive.

He lets me fall asleep, gets his clothes, silently, and leaves before morning; he sleeps better in his bed. He hopes it doesn't bother me; no, not at all, I prefer it. My awakenings are my own.

'Let's meet up in the daytime,' he says. 'It would be funny to see each other in daylight.'

I say yes, but I'm in no hurry to complicate our relationship. In the daytime we can always talk on the phone.

There isn't much written about photography, so I find some books on visual representation instead, which I read, thinking about his work.

He calls in the middle of the afternoon when I'm at the agency. He's on the verge of tears: he doesn't want to do just any old thing, for money. He can manage without money, he's on his own. His only real expense is photographic paper – he can go and eat at his mother's. 'But God, I can't do everything that wanker says, I'll die. Is it normal to feel like crying so often over something stupid, like which lens to use? Do you always have to bow your head and say yes when you want to say no? Why do you have to be sensible the whole time – you know what the going rate is for a day's work, you should know, you've been working long enough, what do I do, do I walk out or keep my mouth shut?'

'You walk out.'

I speak quickly, in a low voice, with my chin just above the desk.

'Listen to me, you have to walk out while you still can. Afterwards it'll be too late and believe me, "too late" is very soon. If you do what he says now, then you'll spend the rest of your life doing what people tell you.'

I'd prefer my belligerent speech not to carry to Anne-Catherine, whose ears are out on stalks. She's sitting opposite me typing, her back to the bay window so she's backlit, her depressive face bent over the keyboard.

'You've got to be strong, and take a risk. If you need money, I'll lend you some. You can pay me back later.'

All this courage I want to give him is the courage I don't have myself. No one ever taught me to say no and soon I'll have been paying the price for fifteen years. It's as though I've got smallpox. My blisters are full of serum: someone only needs to ask, and I'm ready with the vaccine.

I put the phone down. Glancing up, I meet Anne-Catherine's eyes.

'You're right,' she says, her face luminous from the screen's glow, 'It's stupid letting yourself get fucked over when you can get out.'

She gives her straw-coloured bob a pretty shake and turns back to her screen. She's writing an information leaflet for a bank.

6

The Christmas lists have made their appearance in the flat. I keep finding the drafts the children have left lying around on various tables and on my desk.

Mme Alvez puts out a little synthetic fir tree in the entrance hall. She opens it out like an umbrella, before standing it up on the tiled floor and hanging unbreakable baubles from the ends of its plastic branches. Thomas spends ages thanking her with convoluted delicacy on his return home from school. She listens to him, very upright, her face impassive, her broom in her hand. Suzanne doesn't say anything; she thinks the Christmas tree is tacky.

Olivia is invited into the concierge's flat for coffee. Mme Alvez has fallen in love with her, as was to be expected, and tells her the story of her sad and austere widow's life.

My parents, who hardly ever ring me, have started leaving regular messages on the answering machine. They're getting ready for Christmas. I don't ring back.

I drag home a tall fir tree with spreading branches and needles that are almost blue, which I bought at the end of the avenue. I pull out the bag of decorations from the bottom of a cupboard, and buy two new painted wooden angels. I wait impatiently for the children to come home from school. We all decorate the flat together. Manuel gives us a hand. Olivia unfolds the stepladder and hangs streamers from the ceiling light.

I've bought mandarins because their scent blends so well with the smell of the fir. After a couple of days the mixture creates the authentic smell of Christmas – sylvan and exotic.

*

Standing in the kitchen, I fiddle with the radio. I want to listen to the
Advent masses — this time with joy and excitement, I hope. This year
will be the year of revelation. Of reconciliation. Of intelligence awakening in the world.

I want to believe that before I had misunderstood because I was too
young, too stupid. This time I'm really going to listen to all the Pope's
cardinals and I'm going to take what they say on board. I shall be done
with the time of ignorance. The time of the covenant will come.

I make a start on the washing-up, knocking back the sermons. But as
the glasses pile up next to the plates, I begin to feel horribly disappointed. Idiotic — everything they say is idiotic. I'm in despair, realizing
that I had understood it all perfectly well before: Catholics just use
words for the way they sound, as incantations. They dash all our hopes.
Not bothering to dry my hands, I search frantically for a music station.

An hour later, having been bored to tears by the banal chat constantly interrupting the music, I think to myself that maybe the
sermons did mean something, that the meaning's just escaped me. I
leave a space to let the expectation and disappointment back in. I'll try
again next year.

> *While she-pherds wa-atch their flocks by night*
> *All se-eated on the gro-ound*
> *The a-angel of the Lord came down*
> *And glo-or . . .*

'Stop!' Suzanne yells in outrage, punching me furiously in the stomach. 'It's so *annoying* when you sing.'

'OK, I'll dance.'

'Please,' she moans, clinging on to me in the hope that that will
immobilize me, '*please* Mum, stop, for me.'

Thomas intervenes.

'What's up with her now, Mum? Have you noticed she's always ordering us about? She won't even let you sing. Why are you doing what she says? Go on, sing!'

For his sake, I break into,

> *The he-eavenly babe you there shall find*
> *To hu-uman view displa-ayed*
> *All me-e . . .*

Stoically, he listens to me for a few minutes, his brow furrowed in consternation. Then he tiptoes out. Alone now, I sing out of tune at the top of my voice.

I buy a science magazine for Thomas. It comes with an insert, a supplement on time, which he studies for hours.

'Imagine,' he says, planting himself in front of me so as to prevent any attempt at flight, 'imagine time as a row of organ pipes . . .'

'No. It's useless. I can't. Go and talk to someone who can understand what you're saying. Why don't you tell your father, he was very good at physics at school.'

Thomas is tenacious. He's immune to rebuffs.

'Don't give up, you'll get it. So, you fill the pipes with water . . .'

'Oh Thomas, it's no good, I'll never be able to see time as a line. For me it's a circle, which we follow round and round. Like Christmas. Christmas comes round every year, and I can't imagine time any other way. Like Christmas and Easter, always coming back.'

He purses his lips and stares at the floor.

'I'm sorry, you're still very young, you can't understand.'

'No I do, I understand.'

I'm doubtful about that. But I'm mistaken.

'Imagine,' he starts again, 'that time is a circle. Now imagine that inside this circle is a row of organ pipes . . .'

The end of term is approaching. Suzanne brings home an excellent quarterly report. Thomas waits a few days before showing us his, which nonetheless credits him with great, if largely underused, potential.

'Have you seen this?' Olivia says, waving the report under my nose.

I raise an eyebrow.

'What?'

'He's exceptionally gifted. Even his teacher has to admit it.'

Behind Olivia, Thomas is smiling at me grimly. They both infuriate me.

'A genius who does sod all,' I point out nastily, 'grows up to be a hopeless case, if he's lucky, and a drunk if he's not.'

Olivia's arm drops to her side. The report falls as well, struck down in mid-triumph.

'Are you saying that because of me?' she says, good-temperedly.

'Oh, Olivia, have I ever said that you did sod all?'

When I get back late in the evening, the answering machine is blinking frantically. The work messages are plentiful and threatening. I have to deliver; it doesn't matter what, just deliver. My clients are like schoolchildren, studious and narrow-minded, they desperately want their update before Christmas – so they can tidy their desks, I suppose.

Next come the messages from my mother who wants to know what my plans are for the holidays; she's already called several times, why haven't I called her back, she has to get organized.

I also pick up a message for Olivia from Yvette.

'Hello, good morning, Madame, this is Yvette, Olivia's half-sister, I'd like to talk to her, if she'd be kind enough to call us back. She's invited to spend Christmas with the family in Cergy. Olivia, get in touch please. Goodbye, Madame, see you soon.'

Olivia listens to the message, scratching her head. She looks pale.

'Oh yeah,' she mumbles, 'I hadn't thought about that. Christmas. Oh, sure, there's my nephew and niece, I'll go . . .'

'What's the matter?' Thomas says. 'Is there something wrong?'

'No,' Olivia says, 'don't worry, it's just about Christmas . . .'

I look at her and recognize our old friend, the one who says yes because she can't say no. But this time, there's no question of abandoning her to her failing. I do for her what I've so often wished someone would do for me: I force her hand.

'Oh no, really! I thought you were coming to my parents'. I need you for the journey. What will I do if you go to your sister's?'

'My half-sister's.'

'Yes, her. I'll have to give her a call — she'll understand that I need you.'

'But what about my course?'

'What about your course? It begins on the twenty-sixth. You can get the train back on the evening on the twenty-fifth, that'll give you plenty of time.'

She pretends to hesitate. Not for very long.

'If it'll help you, then of course I'll say yes. Yes.'

It's time to ring my mother. I pick up the phone and announce our impending arrival.

7

In the last week of Advent, Denis decides to go away on a trip. His work is being exhibited in a distant capital city, the Foreign Office will pay for his travel, he can stay with a friend, he'll be glad to leave Paris. He's been working a lot, taking pictures of deserted countryside; his photographs have integrity, they stand up to scrutiny. He develops them at night, in his bathroom. He's meticulous, and sure of himself, and broke.

The evening before his flight, when the children are in bed, I leave Olivia in charge of the flat and go round to his place. We check off the contents of his suitcase and he suggests I choose a couple of his photographs for myself. I pick two self-portraits in which he's posing with affected elegance in the middle of a field.

I need money badly. My bank manager keeps calling me and I've just torn my overdraft statement to shreds. On the back of a notebook I make a list of all the people I've worked for recently and add up the money they owe me. It's enough to get me through December. Relieved, I lay down my pencil and pick up the phone. If I don't insist, most of them will never get round to paying me. So I start making calls. I plead. I play the unfortunate woman.

Olivia has been ignoring me for the last few days. She hovers feverishly next to the phone.

'I'm expecting a call,' she says.

The call comes, she answers in a low voice and then disappears for the night. She leaves me to work on my own. I'm angry with her for not keeping the conversation going between us, like a lovely fire. I chain myself to my desk and pound away at the computer all evening, emptying cans of beer and cursing the screen.

Even when I bump into her, she doesn't seem to see me. She comes and goes between her room and the flat. She opens and closes the fridge. She puts on records and doesn't listen to them. She tidies and untidies and tidies up again. When she's done enough aimless roaming about, she gets out the ironing board, piles up the washing, turns on the iron and then wanders off and forgets it. It sits, neglected, shooting out great jets of steam.

She doesn't sit down at the trestle table any more, with the ashtray in front of her, as a prelude to little chats. She only talks to me in passing.

'A clown,' she says, with a preoccupied grimace, 'is laughter and that's all I'm good for, laughter. Just ask Étienne Varlat – I turn everything that happens to me into a joke. That's why people like me. I'm so glad I'm doing this course, I really want to make a go of it . . .'

Her voice affects me like the sound of a mountain spring. It wakes me up and enchants me. I stop working and get up from my desk, I follow her round the flat, everything she says interests me. In all the palpable substance of her body, in all the evanescent substance of her soul, I can't find a single thing that bores me, and, God knows, people are generally a pain in the neck. Trotting along behind her, I offer brief, encouraging words: this course is a godsend, it's great, you're starting to make plans for the future, short term plans maybe, but still, even so, plans for the future.

After one of our peripatetic conversations, I join the local library. Under my name, Olivia takes out books about the circus which she never opens.

'Olivia, a guy called Benoît left a message for you. He wants you to call him back.'

Olivia ignores me. She walks across the room with the Monopoly set in her arms and the children glued to her heels.

'Also, someone keeps hanging up without leaving a message. It's clogging up the answerphone. Have you any idea who it might be?'

She unfolds the board, muttering. The phone rings, and she jumps up on her chair.

'Olivia, it's for you, it's Xavier.'

She snatches the receiver and shuts the living-room door behind her. Through the glass door I can see her murmuring into the phone. Her face is turned to the floor and shielded by her hair.

I take the washing out of the dryer. I pull out a minuscule pair of hemstitched black velvet knickers, a frilly little number from rue Saint-Denis. It's no use trying to fold those things up. I put them away amongst her baggy T-shirts and her worn-out bobby socks.

We've arranged to meet on the morning of Christmas Eve at Gare du Nord, next to the ticket-punching machine at the head of the platform. Laurent is dragging a big bag behind him and Thomas and Suzanne keep sneaking sly, covetous looks at it. He hasn't shut the bag properly, so you can just make out the gleam of the presents' iridescent wrapping paper and the colourful froth of their ribbons.

'Have you got presents for everyone? Even us?' Suzanne asks in a honeyed voice, so unlike her usual booming, husky tones.

'Ho, ho, ho!' roars Laurent.

The children elbow each other, smirking. They flank Laurent adoringly and stick to him like leeches. We get on the train.

Olivia is meticulously made up. She doesn't say a word, just smiles bashfully. After I've sat down, I count the tickets again, checking that they've been punched and that the reservations are right. I sink into my seat. Hmmm, Christmas.

*

My parents are hospitable and garrulous. About ten years ago, they instigated a sort of superabundant Christmas; they invite forty people, cook for sixty, and lay on enough drink for eighty. Between nine and twelve on Christmas Eve about fifty people of all different types and ages turn up at their house, a mixture of familiar faces, friends and close relatives. The feast takes place largely between the fireplace in the living room and the sideboard in the dining room; the double doors between the two rooms are kept open and the kitchen is used as an annexe. The chattering guests enact a slow choreography. Groups form and dissolve like the changing patterns in a kaleidoscope. The children stampede about in a frenzy of excitement. Towards midnight some of the guests who were born in the sixties go up to the bedrooms to take drugs. They come back down wearing smiles like slices of watermelon and the evening continues. The older guests have drunk so much that they don't see any of this. Even if they hadn't been drinking, which is an appealing theory, I still don't think they'd notice anything out of the ordinary. They're amiable enough, but they've never been very attentive.

For music, we play Easy-Listening. The English Christmas numbers at the start of the evening are followed by American tunes from the fifties and sixties. When it's my turn to choose, I put on Stan Getz, which is received with contented indifference.

The party goes on and on. Nobody leaves until the cellar's been drunk dry. In the fireplace, the fire devours a tonne of wood. In the morning the electric coffee-maker gives up the ghost under the strain and someone has to go and borrow one from next door.

It always takes at least three days for the festivities to play themselves out. Eventually everyone has a migraine and a hangover. People begin to gather up their presents, and those who aren't staying at the house stop coming round. My parents put a last load into the dishwasher, count up the number of empty bottles in the cellar and settle down in front of the telly for a little snooze. Christmas is declared over until next year.

Olivia finds her own place among the good-natured groups. With a glass of champagne in one hand and a cigarette in the other, she introduces herself to everybody. She's wearing a sparkling black blouse; her earrings dangle against her neck and she looks ravishing. I give it an hour before everyone has got to know her and like her. I abandon her to the general goodwill. And I abandon myself to the giddying round of brief conversations, keeping one eye out for my children in case they get into conversation with a proselytizing adult who's keen to explain to them exactly what sort of family they belong to.

I forget Olivia, which is a mistake. She's made new friends. At midnight she disappears upstairs to the bedrooms.

When I find her again, it's two o'clock in the morning and she wants to go to bed; she wants to be at her best for her course. She was hoping to slip away quietly, but I grab her at the bottom of the stairs. She stands sheepishly on the second step. I stand on the doormat and point a vengeful finger at her, trembling with anger.

'I swear,' she murmurs plaintively, 'I swear I didn't take anything.'

'Are you having me on? Everyone else was taking drugs and you just watched and didn't touch anything?'

'I didn't, I promise. Anyway, they were smoking and I'm not into that.'

'They were smoking? At *Christmas*? Do you think I'm a total idiot?'

'Alright. OK. But I don't like acid, either.'

'So are we allowed to know why you went upstairs with them?'

'Because they were nice. Anyway, you can ask them. They'll tell you I didn't take anything.'

'*Me*? Do you really think they're going to tell *me* the truth?'

She is holding her presents. I gave her a pair of knee-length silk shorts and a sleeveless top. My mother gave her a silver ring in the shape of a daisy. She stands motionless and contrite in the face of my fury. Occasionally she sneaks a shifty look at me. I've worn out my reproaches and my voice is breaking. She smiles wretchedly. My God, I could swear she's loving this. My anger disintegrates; I feel like laughing and wishing her a good night. But I don't do either. Instead, I raise my voice. 'I'm warning you that if I catch you getting up to any of this sort of stuff again, then it's over, do you understand? Over. Now go on, go to bed. You know your course starts the day after tomorrow.'

She turns her back on me and nips up the stairs on tiptoe, ascending as quickly and lightly as a fun-fair balloon. With my hands on my hips, I contemplate the empty staircase severely.

The station is deserted. A ray of light still glazes the waste ground beside the tracks. Looking across the rails the view on the other side is blocked off by some bricked-up houses. Sections of red brick are beginning to collapse in places. A smell of stone and fire announces the fall of evening. The air crunches a little. The ice muffles sound. I hop from foot to foot. Thick, slow tears from the cold inch down my cheeks. I jangle the car keys to warm up my fingertips. Olivia clutches her bag to her stomach.

'That was fun,' she says. 'They're nice, your family.'

'Yeah, yeah.'

I feel calmer, but I'm not appeased. Last night's alcoholic excess has altered my mood.

'Hey,' Olivia adds, 'it wasn't my fault. It was your cousin who started me off about drugs. He was asking me loads of questions. Then he even asked for my phone number.'

'Did you give it to him?'

'No, I gave him yours. He was disappointed. He went on and on about it but I told him I didn't have my own phone. He said he'd write to me.'

She looks at me proudly. She tells on my cousin as a three-year-old would, as a token of her good faith and the price of keeping up our alliance. I answer her roughly.

'Fine. From now on, I've got a good reason to fall out with him.'

She panics, sensing injustice.

'Because he takes drugs?'

'No, because he's getting me mixed up in his shit. Because he's getting you mixed up in it. Because I'm responsible for you.'

We take a step back as the train arrives. It comes round the bend, its great pale eyes boring holes in the overgrown hedges at each side of the track.

'Have you got the keys to the flat? Check you've got them!'

Anticipating the excruciating scream of the brakes, I put my hands over my ears. Olivia yells, 'Hey, I meant to ask, do you believe me now, that I didn't take anything?'

We walk hurriedly down the line of carriages.

'Yes, I believe you. You've got no idea how much I believe you. I trust you to death.'

'That's nice,' she whispers.

'It's not nice at all. I haven't got a choice, dummy.'

She gets into the carriage and finds her seat. She waves at me through the window. The train pulls out of the station. I walk alongside it for a second or two and shout, 'Don't forget to lock the door in the morning when you leave!'

Then, treading carefully, I go back to the car with my hands in my pockets. It's dark, it's nearly teatime, my feet are frozen and I want to kiss my children.

8

I walk through the deserted rooms for a long time. I can feel my soul expanding, a gas or a vapour which stretches and spreads and fills all the space between these walls. The slightest image knocks into it and resonates. I have to be very careful not to allow the echoes to deafen me.

Cracks open in my heart when I come across a broken toy left lying on the floor, dirty plates piled up in the sink, a jersey thrown over the back of the sofa. Delicious tears rise and die away at the edge of my throat.

I reach the end of the passage, and, overwhelmed, take a look in the children's bedroom. I turn and walk through the flat in the opposite direction. I go into the bathroom and turn on the bath tap. I'm not too sure what to do with my body. I'm going to soak it and soften it, soap it carefully and then dry it. I'm going to think of this body as my twin and attempt to lodge myself in its friendly skin, and stay there.

We took the train this morning and arrived back in Paris at lunchtime. Jean-Patrick came to fetch the children in the middle of the afternoon. Their backpacks were still lying in the doorway. From our many years of conjugal life he has retained a touching way of entering my home. He behaves exactly as if it was his. He has an imperious way of installing his tall person on my premises and taking a proprietorial look at my disorder which I'm very fond of. I – who have so much trouble trying to make my practical body and my vaporous soul coexist – I am grateful for anything that binds and unifies me, including the look yesterday's husband gives today's curtains.

They left. I adored, as I did every time, the peaceful gesture of shutting the door, of closing off my home, of closing off myself. The lock made a high, springy noise accompanying my voice. Bye, darlings, bye, click. I can no longer see them. I lean my face against the door panel and rest my forehead on the white-painted wood.

I listen to the domestic silence. It gives me a feeling of conspiratorial glee, this confirmation of what I already know: when the children have gone, I'm on my own.

My bed calls me. It says, you should lie down when you get the chance and sleep, that sleep is the reward of women who get divorced. I'm useless at resisting direct invitations; I haven't even got to my room before my body is already full of drowsiness, a stream of endorphins washing through my veins and my head fogging up with dreams. I lie down and close my eyes, seeking out warmth. Then I curl up under the rumpled duvet and fall asleep. There we are, evening is drawing in and I sleep the sleep of the blessed.

When I wake up I'm disorientated. No one's waiting for me to cook their supper, no one's asking me to go out and buy bread or milk, no one needs me to put them to bed before ten o'clock, with their teeth and their imagination freshly brushed. It's nearly dark but no one's turned a light on in the flat. I have a bath. I didn't think I'd miss Olivia so much.

She wasn't here this morning when we got home; the door was double-locked. I shouldn't wait for her, the course is bound to end late and she'll probably go and eat with her new friends afterwards – that's what I'd do if I was her. I wait all the same. I speculate: if I work late enough, she'll turn up in the end. She'll probably drop by the flat before going up to her room, she might like to have a cup of coffee with me, or a chat, who knows.

I get out of the bath and dress mechanically. I look on my desk for my files and set up the computer on the trestle table. The hours pass.

There's no sign of Olivia. I drink a cup of coffee on my own and go to bed, feeling lost. I fall asleep instantly. I dream that I discover a new door in my flat. It opens onto passages I never knew were there. Walking down them I pass rooms hung with mildewed red velvet. I push open a door and find myself in a bright room. Giant insects sway gently back and forth at head height, dozing in grey silk cocoons suspended by thick white threads.

I must have been waiting so intently in my sleep that the faint sound of footsteps drag me out of bed more effectively than a battery of alarm clocks. It's not quite seven a.m. I dash to the kitchen, tense and terribly alert. There're two of them, sitting opposite each other at the yellow plastic table. They're dressed, their hair's done and they're ready for the day. They are having their breakfast. It's wonderful.

'Oh hi, morning.'

I reply with a bland, almost indifferent 'morning', despite feeling an almost irresistible desire to break into a little dance of reunion on the cold tiles.

'Have a chair,' Olivia says, civilly, 'sit down, I'll get you a cup of coffee. This is Amélie, she's on the course with me. She's from Rennes. She didn't have anywhere to sleep so we both squeezed into my room. She's a Whiteface clown. I'm more of an Auguste. It all depends on your personality, what type of clown you are. I've thought about it a lot.'

'Good morning, Amélie.'

I incline my head courteously. I must look very peculiar to her, with my hair sticking up in tufts, skimpily dressed in a hundred-year-old sweat shirt and an ancient pair of knickers. I sit down and cross my legs under the table.

'Good morning, Madame.'

Amélie has the clear face of a young girl who has been brought up in the fresh air. She has the direct, pleasant gaze, the bland smile, the pale, neatly pulled back hair, the calm manner, and, my God, I could swear she has the look of stupidity, too. Hmmm, yes, in fact I'd stake my life that she's a silly goose: even half awake, I can still spot a silly goose. How alive my Olivia looks, next to her; how beautiful; how effortlessly she distinguishes herself from the inert matter around her, the tables, the walls and the boxes of washing powder.

'I wonder,' Olivia chatters on, 'what Dominique's after. At the beginning he was always putting me down, I thought he couldn't stand me. But then yesterday he was so nice. He must've spent two hours showing me how to do those movements I couldn't get the hang of, you know, the very slow ones.'

Amélie says nothing. She nods in agreement and breaks her biscuit into hundreds of tiny pieces which she then stuffs nimbly into her mouth. She opens and closes her mouth countless times, with electrifying speed, like a little fledgling. What a strange, hypocritical way of eating, at once voracious and unbearably prissy. I watch, fascinated. Olivia continues to muse about the course, at the top of her voice.

'At first I thought I'd get on better with Anne-Marie, but now I'm keener on Dominique – he seems more serious, he used to work with the Grüss circus, you know. What do you think, Amélie?'

Amélie doesn't think much. It's seven thirty. I upend the coffee pot over my cup but there're only a few drops left. Olivia gets up from the table.

'It's time, come on, let's go. By the way, there's an end-of-course show on Friday evening, it's at nine o'clock. I've reserved a seat for you, can you come?'

'Of course.'

I beam at her. I'm not quick enough to make the connection: this

Friday evening, the night of the performance, is the same Friday evening as New Year's Eve.

Olivia and Amélie pick up their bags and coats and set off, two studious early risers, two young students in a university town which has hundreds of thousands of students.

9

Soon we will have been waiting on the director's floor of the bank for an hour. We're in a little vestibule in the middle of a corridor, opposite the PR office.

Mylène is exasperated. She's not in the habit of hiding her feelings. Sunk in an armchair that's too deep for her, she furiously crosses and uncrosses her legs, her winter coat hanging half open. The skirt of her suit rides up her thighs, the Lycra whistling softly against her legs.

What on earth are those shoes she's gone and bought herself? Designer footwear like that belongs in a shop window – no one actually walks around in it.

Patrick and I stand opposite her and listen in silence. I hold myself with my chest pushed forward, hoping that this wading-bird pose will divert attention away from my own shoes; one of the heels is badly worn and the leather is terribly stained. These shoes had it months ago. Why don't I ever get round to buying a new pair? I'm pathetic. And if only I'd got round to tucking in the thread dangling off the belt of my cagoule.

Mylène has sent me home to change more than once. She expects me to be present at a certain number of meetings with her clients, and at these meetings she does not expect my clothes to insult the majesty of her shoes or that of the people we're speaking to. The banker, the engineer, the advertising executive, the press attaché — they're all extremely sensitive people. Carelessness in one's dress pierces them through the heart and consequently, the wallet, which beats demurely so close, so close to that tender organ.

Mylène gives me a wan look. She's trembling slightly.

'No way,' she says, looking me up and down.

I look down at myself. I see a pullover and a pair of trousers. The pullover is slightly faded. I don't look at my shoes, I wish my feet would disappear.

'God, you could at least have made an effort.'

Patrick rolls his eyes. He's scarcely better dressed than I am, and what's more he's insolent, but he's a man, lucky sod. The minute a man's had a shave, regardless of whether he actually possesses any real qualities, he can always pass for intelligent. Besides, Mylène, who loves being brutal to women, derives less pleasure from treating men harshly. So Patrick doesn't give a damn about her moods.

'What's the problem this time?' he says haughtily.

I'd like to snuggle up against his great big black leather jacket.

'Èvelyne Carrier. I had her on the phone yesterday evening, she's furious. She can't understand how you would dare to submit something so badly written. The chairman gave it back to her with everything crossed out. Apparently, you didn't even use *verbs* in some of the sentences. She thinks the whole thing will have to be redone.'

'What's she mean, it's all got to be redone?' says Patrick. 'He can just stick his precious verbs in himself, the silly old fart.'

'Keep your voice down, please. The silly old fart is the head of the bank. I'm the one who's in the shit here. I run this company, I'm responsible for the profit margin and there's a lot of money tied up in this book.'

If she hadn't been wearing so much lipstick, she'd be biting her lips. She is furious.

'I'm going to have to start reading through everything that leaves the agency, if this carries on . . .'

'How much money?' Patrick interrupts.

'Don't be so petty, that's got nothing to do with you. I can't afford to lose a client, that's all. I've got shareholders.'

'Anyway,' Patrick remarks, 'I'm not rewriting this pile of crap for nothing.'

For a second I get the thrilling impression that Mylène is going to jump out of her armchair and slap him full in the face, but then the door to the office suddenly swings open.

Èvelyne Carrier emerges. From the look of her footwear, she goes to the same shoe shop as Mylène. I've had it.

'Good morning, Èvelyne!'

Mylène bounds to her high-heeled feet. She pulls her skirt down briskly to her plump little knees. She looks straight at Èvelyne, flashing a lethal smile which is instantly belied by the promise of capitulation in her eyes. She marches ahead of us, her head held high.

We follow – Patrick, me, my shoes and my cagoule. Taking dainty steps (another diversionary tactic) I go into the office. I sit down at a giant's table on a giant's chair. The view through the picture window takes in the whole of the Champs Élysées.

Èvelyne Carrier sits at the top of the table in the powdery winter light. She contemplates us wordlessly for a moment, her elegant chin in her baby-soft hands. On either side of her, two tall henchmen in shirts and ties observe a melancholy silence, looking into the middle distance. They share her disapproval.

'So,' she asks, her voice icy, 'what happened?'

Mylène presses her mohair bust towards her.

'It was a briefing problem, Èvelyne. There was a misunderstanding. But I can guarantee you my editors' full attention. They're going to go over the whole book from start to finish. All you'll have to do is correct them. That's what they're there for.'

Normally it doesn't matter what we write – it's never going to be read, anyway. Which is a stroke of luck and I use it in my defence. In fact I'm going to use it in my defence when the Last Judgement comes and I'm called upon to account for my actions.

'Everyone lied,' I will say to the prosecutor in the plumed hat, 'you have to remember that. But *my* lies, sir, never fooled anyone. I promise you no one ever read a line of anything I wrote. In these circumstances, can you reasonably charge me with having degraded my fellow man?'

I'm well aware of the wretchedness of this line of argument. The prosecutor will have a field day censuring the trivialization of injustice, the way lying has become an employee of the state. I will search my past for any evidence of resistance to the triumph of market forces. To no avail. It'll turn out that I've done nothing with my time except collaborate with the enemy and polish its trumpets.

But I won't panic. Just when he's worked up a good head of steam, he'll go too far. I'll seize my chance. Shedding a few tears, I'll remind him that it was a sad, confused time. I'll denounce the sleeping partners and the leading profiteers, I'll put it to the court that I was defenceless and depressed. I'll call my bank manager to the stand, who'll testify that I was always overdrawn and never received alimony. She'll refute the charge of personal gain. I'll solicit their contempt in order to exonerate me of the offence.

It'll be a nasty moment but I'm sure I'll save my skin. Honestly, I believe I'll get the minimum. For giving false evidence. For aiding and abetting fraud. Maybe for ordering food and drink in restaurants and not being able to pay for it, as well.

Patrick and I had worked together on the book. It was meant to celebrate the bank's centenary. We had shared the chapters – he did the story up to 1945, and I took it on from there. Now Mylène and Èvelyne share the cane. We spend an interminable amount of time condemning our sentences, we murmur lengthy apologies, we promise a thousand times to respect verbs in future; all those beautiful conjugated verbs without which language is nothing but hideous gibberish. Before becoming a PR for the bank, Èvelyne worked in publishing, a fact she reminds us of frequently. She did indeed; yes, in publishing, she knows what is fit to be called syntax.

We strike out the chapters: first 1936 to 1939, then 1939 to 1945, then 1954 to 1962, then 1968, then all the 80s. What can I say about your disgraceful version of our bank's history, my God, what can I say without being insulting? *Surely* you can see that there's a question of interpretation here – even the finest historians can't see eye to eye. And can we please get rid of that ridiculous rant – war is a terrible shame, but there it is, that's war.

I'm dying for a beer. Obsessively, I make notes of every nuance of Èvelyne Carrier's speech. I'm planning, shamelessly, to serve them back to her – there's nothing people enjoy quite as much as their own reheated inanities.

'We're such idiots,' says Patrick as we walk across the bank's vast lobby. 'We should've seen that coming. That's what happens when someone pays you to do their dirty work.'

Mylène is sulking. She thinks we're snobby and pretentious. She detests us this morning. She hitches her skirt up to get into the taxi which is waiting for her at the foot of the building. *Crisss*, go her stockings. She doesn't say goodbye.

'She's angry,' I say.

'It'll pass,' answers Patrick, 'as soon as the cheque arrives.'

I ask Patrick if he wants a beer. In the café he tells me that he's working a lot at the moment, nothing very exciting, he'd like to do his own writing, but he's been too busy preparing to go to Mali with his eldest son, and he's just moved into a new flat. He doesn't think the rewriting will take very long.

'It's easy, you just have to take out half the text with a red pen and then bung in verbs all over the place with a black one. There's only one important question, as far as I can see: how are we going to screw some more money out of Mylène?'

On the way to the Metro, he recommends I read *1793*. He's just split up with his girlfriend, a lovely, endearing girl with very brown, almost black hair who we've worked with for years. He's philosophical about the break-up. I'm not. I miss the couple they used to make. It's funny the way I become attached to certain partnerships.

10

Damn, I can't get used to the empty flat. My coffee cup is in the same place I left it this morning. There's a black ring congealed on the saucer. The hours have passed and no angel has had the grace to change the cup's position, move it out of the way or even break it. It's indifferent and immobile, fossilized. Suzanne. Thomas. Olivia. I miss their unambiguous mess.

I find a message from Thierry on the answering machine. Oh. Thierry. I try to remember his telephone number and realize with some pleasure that I've forgotten it. I look it up in the phonebook. I'm not interested in pointless revenge – I do what the faint voice on the machine has asked me, and call him immediately. Can he come over, now, to my place? Yes. He's on his way. See you soon.

As I wait for him, the cup catches my eye again. I pick it up and go into the kitchen. The cup slides off the saucer and crashes onto the floor, leaving a little brown oil slick. The coffee wasn't as petrified as I thought, this morning isn't as distant from this evening as I thought; time is smaller than it seems.

I get down on my knees and make a few desultory sweeps at the fragments with the hand brush. I thought time would separate the two of us, but nothing has congealed there, either. It's as though Thierry went out as usual, this morning – perhaps he had things to do – and now here he is coming home in the evening.

I tip the shards of the coffee cup into the bin and put the brush away under the sink. Imagine that time is a circle and now imagine that inside this circle there's a row of organ pipes filled with water . . .

'Christmas,' says Thierry, 'was sort of the problem.'

He hasn't taken off his white canvas jacket or his printed scarf. He's plonked himself straight down on the edge of the sofa, wedging his clasped hands between his knees.

Maybe he shouldn't have gone to his parents' but he didn't want to let his mother down. He should be more careful: feeling sorry for his parents is a costly business. There's never any pleasure to be had from it in the end, just a bill. He's mad at himself for always forgetting how badly his father beat him until he grew big enough to stop it; his father used to hit them as hard as he could, and call his mother a whore and the children pigs. His memory is a maze, he keeps losing his way. He's barely gone down a path before the thickets have grown back behind him. When he turns round to survey his progress, he doesn't recognize anything, he's full of doubts. 'My father's a bastard,' he always claims – but maybe he's the bastard, how can he be sure?

He thinks that he can go back to his parents' house with impunity, he thinks he'll feel at home there. It's a terrible mistake, but he never remembers this until he crosses the threshold.

When he got there, they were already sitting at the table: all of them – his father and his mother and his sister and his aunt and the two cousins with their wives and children. No one was exchanging presents, presents are for children and the children were going to open them the next day. 'Christmas is on the twenty-fifth until it's proved otherwise!' shouted the old man. 'At least there's one of our traditions that's still legal!'

'*Our traditions*,' Thierry repeated laughing. He'd already drunk a lot before he'd arrived, and he carried on.

They all talked at his parents' – the father talked, the cousins talked. Thierry didn't say anything. His family is Catholic. After the fish, they talked about religion. 'Fucking Semites,' said the old man. The cousins laughed, their flabby necks creasing into folds, they loved that kind of stuff.

There are many Semites in the world, Arabs and Jews, and if you're so inclined there's plenty to say about them. When it's all been said, you can always start again at the beginning. Hatred cements people, it lays the foundations for friendships, it's a source of recognition. Hatred's a bit of a slut, but she's a good girl, really.

'What a lovely dinner.'

'At least it's none of that Arab shit,' said one cousin.

'Yeah, roll on the Final Solution,' said the other cousin.

*

'Shut your face!' Thierry had said.

His eyes were stinging, they were probably all red. His voice was nasal. It's weird how drink makes your voice come out through your nose.

He wasn't looking for a fight, he just wanted the racket to stop – the noise of their talking was preventing him from taking peaceful refuge in drink, which is a place, not a feeling, solitary and silent. But the old man flew off the handle. He pushed back his chair and stood up, banging his fist on the table. Everyone thought he was going to hit his son. The cousins were happy. Everyone looked up from their food. The moment before a beating always seems to go on for ever, Thierry remembered clearly then.

'Get out!' his father yelled.

But then he sat back down in his chair. He is very old, now. He said again, without shouting this time, 'Get out, faggot.'

Thierry's mother was crying by now, which didn't mean anything, she was always crying. Thierry picked up a bottle from the table and left. He didn't say goodbye. He drank the bottle on the stairs, thinking how stupid he was to have ruined his evening. Then he walked home.

He started laughing. His father could easily have knocked him down if he'd smacked him round the head – he was so drunk he would have fallen over if someone had breathed on him. Then he started crying. He was sorry he'd gone to his parents', sorry his father wasn't dead yet – although he wasn't even very sure about that, a dead father might be even more of a burden than a living father, even a bastard of a living father. The problem was simply having a father at all.

When he got home a young guy was hanging around outside the door of his building, who Thierry knew by sight. He was pleased to see

him. He took hold of his arm and led him up to his flat. The guy prepared a fix. Thierry turned out his drawers and found himself a
syringe, a little ten-franc syringe which dated from his pre-reformed
days. The young guy said, 'That's better. Happy Christmas.' He was
HIV positive.

The spoon was the problem. Neither of them thought about the
spoon, they were so drunk. They shared the same one.

'It's so stupid,' says Thierry. 'Now I've got to wait three months for the
results of the test.

'God,' I say. 'Just your average Christmas, then.'

He looks crestfallen.

'You can say that again,' he murmurs.

He hangs his head, resting his forehead in his interlaced fingers.

'Mind you, at least you only shared the spoon.'

'You don't know anything about it,' he says, wearily.

'No, you're right, I don't, thank God. Anyway, put on a record, I'll
make some tea.'

I stand up. I must be careful not to absorb the information too
quickly. Thought is a slow horse. I get up to put the kettle on. I plant
a kiss on Thierry's forehead as I walk past on my way to the kitchen.

We go back over the whole business, discussing it and hesitating
over what should bear the brunt of the responsibility. I say the family.
He says the drink. I say the drugs. Finally, we agree to pin it all on
religion.

Our bodies are fitted together, his chest against my back, his arms
round my shoulders. I make a spiritual exercise out of trying to feel the
soft grain of his skin. He sleeps, squeezing me up with my face against
the wall. I listen to his breathing on the back of my neck.

When we wake up, he tells me his dream. He was walking slowly down a mountain road, knowing that he was on his way to meet someone. The road was bordered with strawberries, wild strawberries, grainy and scarlet. It brought him to a waterfall but there was no one waiting for him there after all. He was surprised to find himself on his own, but he felt no anxiety, only a slight dizziness tempered by the sweet memory of the strawberries. That's all.

I pick up a pad of paper from my desk and tear off a page. I write, 'There is no one at the waterfall, but there are strawberries on the road.'

We come out of my room. It is still very early. Olivia and Amélie are in the kitchen, finishing their coffee. Olivia catches sight of Thierry behind me, barefoot, his head bent as he buttons up his trousers.

'Well,' she says gleefully, slapping the table, 'how about that for a surprise! Thierry's back! Great! . . . Take a seat, honeybun. Coffee?'

She jams half a loaf of bread in the toaster. Wedged up tight against the element, it quickly browns and smoke billows out of the toaster. Olivia blows on it, unperturbed. She makes jokes, she bustles about; she's giving him a warm welcome. I'm glad I've brought Thierry back home for us. I love gratifying Olivia's legitimism. I, too, regret separations.

I I

God, it's so cold. The wind sweeps painful tears onto my cheeks. Luckily it's blowing a gale, or these tears would freeze and I'd die a wretched death, my eyes iced over in an unknown land. Why does the night become so black, so wild, and so silent the minute you leave the womb of Paris? Why is there nobody about? These streets all look the same, what the hell have I done with Olivia's map? It will soon be nine o'clock on New Year's Eve and I'm completely lost in some nameless, deathly suburb.

There's never a reward. I took the Metro to the end of the line, crossed the dismal no-man's-land of bus stops, ignored the signs and jumped the barriers and charged down the boulevard, risking my life. I entered this labyrinth of suburban streets and closes willingly enough, and I've ended up wandering through them for hours. Must I really die of exhaustion? On the eve of a new year? All because Olivia invited me to her end-of-course show?

I plant myself under a street light. I open my bag and fish out a scrap of paper which I smooth flat. I rotate the map. I retrace my steps. A paper lantern flickers in a doorway. I've found it.

The show's in a loft hung with black cloth. The banks of wooden seats are full. Families, a few children and enthusiastic friends slap their hands together vigorously to try and quell the imperious cold. The four braziers are having no effect. I try my hardest not to look round. I saw Yvette come in with her husband and the two kids a few minutes ago. They pushed aside the heavy curtain screening the performance space and edged their way into the tiers of seats. They're sitting two rows behind me. I curl up. With any luck, they won't see me and they'll leave before the end of the show so I won't have to say hello.

'Is that you?'

The voice trickles into my ear. I toy with saying, You've made a mistake, Madame, I think you've got me mixed up with somebody else, good evening. Instead I feign joy and amazement. 'Yvette!' I bawl.

She jumps backwards, stricken.

'What a nice surprise,' she whispers, 'don't move, we'll come and join you.'

The light fades gently as Olivia's family come and plonk themselves down in my row. It goes dark. I stare fixedly at the stage in front of me.

'I loathe shows,' I say to Cécile the next day. We're having a drink in an almost deserted café. 'The only bit I like is when the lights go back up. Once the stage empties, the curtain falls and the audience gets to its feet, I can escape. Which is a total relief. I don't like the way shows make fun of the world, I don't like the shamelessness of the actors. They take us hostage, they can make us watch painful things . . .'

'Do you think?' says Cécile, but she's not listening. She lets me rattle on as she watches the reflections of the few loafers who push open the door of the café in the mirror opposite. She's hoping to catch sight of someone she knows.

'And yet,' I say, determined to finish my story despite her indifference, 'when Olivia stepped into the circle of light, the shambolic theatre fell silent. I knew immediately she was going to be brilliant. Before she came on, I kept looking at my watch, but I pulled my sleeve down over it during her bit. I stopped wanting the show to be over for a while. She was fantastic. She sent shivers up your spine.'

'How are the kids?' Cécile interrupts me.

'They're fine, I guess. They're at Jean-Patrick's.'

It's disconcerting, the way people always ask me for news of the children. They couldn't care less when I talk about Olivia. They never ask after her, or wonder what her news is. And yet they know perfectly well that we live together.

*

I decide to walk home. If I go by the backstreets, I'm bound to find a shop that's open on the way. I need milk and cereal. Cécile pushes her bike beside me.

'I don't know about Thierry,' she says, 'but my ex told me the stupidest lie. He's never shared a syringe in his life. I should have guessed. I mean, he's so squeamish, there's no way he'd ever inject himself with anything. The thing was, he'd slept with some girl who it turned out was waiting for the results of her HIV test. Of course, he had to tell me, it affected me too. So he made up this whole scenario: he thought that if he admitted he'd slept with someone, the shit would really hit the fan, so instead he told me he'd shared a fix with a friend . . . But he couldn't help letting the truth out pretty soon afterwards. "It's your fault!" he said. "You *made* me lie." All that rigmarole, and in the end he turns out to be negative!'

'Still,' I say, 'It's strange the things people come up with. It reminds me of Jean-Pierre, one of Agnès's old boyfriends. He was always disappearing without warning. One evening, he left her in a restaurant – he asked her out and then never turned up. Next morning he tells her that he spent the night in the sack with some guy he picked up in a club.

'"Do you think I'm a complete idiot?" Agnès said to him, "You've never looked at a guy in your life!"

'"OK, OK, I admit it. It wasn't a guy, it was two girls. I picked them up in a bar in Pigalle. We went to a hotel. I made it up about the guy so you wouldn't be jealous. Do you forgive me?"

'"You can get fucked," Agnès said. "Get your stuff and piss off."

'"Alright! Don't get so worked up! That stuff about the two girls is rubbish. What actually happened was I stayed the night at Carol's. I went round there in the early evening and she was really depressed. I didn't think she should spend the night on her own so I stayed. But

I thought that two whores wouldn't hurt you as much as one Carol. That's it, it's all over. Now do you forgive me?"'

'Great!' Cécile says. 'So what about you? Do you believe in this Christmas fix, then?'

The white light on the stage fades and the yellow light comes on above the rows of seats. I stand up abruptly and push past Yvette.

'Sorry, I have to go the toilet.'

I elbow my way through some of the audience blocking the door of the loft and catch sight of a guy dressed up as a clown.

'I'm looking for Olivia.'

'Downstairs. She's in the kitchen, taking off her make-up.'

I find Olivia sitting down with her hair up and her face covered in cream. She's in the middle of an animated discussion with her colleagues. I don't want to interrupt.

I tear a page out of my address book and scribble a few words. I thrust the note at a girl stamping her feet in the passage.

'Please could you give this to that young woman in there, the one who's laughing. Yes, sitting down with her hair tied back.'

I go back down the corridor and open the front door. The black street of identical houses stretches in front of me. It's eleven thirty, impenetrably dark and the Metro is a long way away. And God, it's so cold.

I am on the Metro at Corentin Cariou. On the seat in front of me a boy is leaning towards a girl, kissing her. I watch his tongue clear her open lips, pass her patient teeth, slowly caress her mouth. If this kiss hadn't already been given, I'd gladly take it. I glance at my watch. It's five to twelve.

At midnight we reach Louis Blanc. No one is kissing any more. The new year has just begun.

*

Half an hour later I meet up with Thierry in Nation. One of Laurent's friends is having a party. Music is pounding out of the first-floor windows; the building might explode if they were closed.

Groups of people are clustered in the courtyard and on the stairs, talking. On the first floor, guests flow in and out through the wide-open doors of the flat. Under the glass roof people are pressed up against each other, dancing. In the kitchen you have to shout to be heard. The bathroom is locked, there's a ray of light coming out from under the door. I catch sight of Laurent. He points to Thierry who's walking down the passage. I catch him by the sleeve. I put my tongue in his mouth.

'Happy New Year, sweetheart.'

He passes me his glass. I go and dance.

12

Suzanne is stretched out on the sofa. I sit down beside her, lift up her jumper and massage her stomach in a circular movement, rotating around her bellybutton. She turns her pale face up to the ceiling and grimaces with pain.

'It hurts,' she groans.

'I know.'

She has been complaining of stomach ache since mid-afternoon. We've almost exhausted our arsenal of remedies: milk of magnesia, Spasfon, the glass of warm water, derision, the Cinderella video, massage. I play my final trump card.

'Ever since you were very little you've turned your worries into stomach pains, do you remember? This time, I think you've got schoolache. You don't feel like going back and starting the new term tomorrow.'

'No, I don't,' she says.

'Come on, it's not that bad.'

She gives me an ulcerated look.

'It is, it is that bad.'

'Well, don't go then. Stay at home with Olivia. I'll give you a note. We'll ask Marion for your homework and you can go back when you're feeling better.'

But Suzanne decides she *does* want to go to school, she categorically wants to go and that's not why she's got a stomach ache. With my hand on her middle, I tell her that I admire her way of giving substance to what's annoying her. We make a list of the different names people give to pains of uncertain origins.

To have a stomach ache.

To have a headache.

To have heartache.

To have a nightmare.

To feel jumpy.

To feel tired.

To be sick.

She thinks that it's hurting a little less. She wants to know what's on the menu for supper.

'Are crêpes good for your stomach?'

It's ten o'clock and Suzanne is asleep. Thomas pushes open the door of the living room.

'I can't sleep,' he says in a weak voice. 'It's awful. I'm bored in bed and I'm going to be really tired tomorrow.'

'Come and sit down next to me. When you're worried about

something you often have trouble getting to sleep, remember? Perhaps it's got something to do with having to go back to school tomorrow . . .'

'You can't say that school's got nothing to do with it, this time.'

Olivia came in a short while ago. She spent the weekend at Cergy. She looks like thunder.

'Admit it. The kids don't suddenly get ill the day before the holidays start, do they?'

'Yes, Olivia. I admit it. No, they don't.'

I've got a bit of a headache myself. The day before the start of term makes me feel apprehensive, as well. I wipe the plywood tray with a sponge. It's covered in sugar, which makes my fingers sticky. I grumble, 'I'd prefer it if we could try not to criticize school too much in front of the children. We can't keep telling them it's a dreadful place and then take them there every morning. If school is that awful, we'll have to take them out and keep them at home.'

'Oh no,' Olivia says brusquely, 'no, no. Children need school. Even boarding school isn't that bad, it depends on the child. You can be very happy at boarding school.'

Olivia is advocating school. It's bizarre. She's praising boarding school, which is even more disturbing. It will soon be eleven o'clock and I don't feel like having any painful conversations. But I can't always postpone everything. So I put the sponge on the table and sit down on the amplifier. I wait.

'It's my sister. My brother-in-law is fucking about with my niece.'

'We were in the kitchen. My sister was making dinner. He was playing with Sophie. He was doing things. He was touching her – in front of my sister – and she was wriggling. I told him, "Stop it, you filthy bastard."

'"Shut up, you pervert," my sister said to me, "you're mad."

'"What's the problem?" said my brother-in-law. "Why are you making a scene, Olivia? Can't you see that she's loving it? Eh, you love it, don't you?"

'He had his hand in her pants. She wasn't saying anything, just looking at her father. Little girls — you should see their eyes, that lying expression, pleased and excited. They're completely defenceless.'

Olivia has a particular way of telling a story. She spares me the details. She shields me from brutalities. She just makes sure I've understood.

That way, she preserves the distance between us. I know she's afraid that the meaning of the story will get lost if it turns into a string of graphic images. She is wary of pornography.

'My sister just bangs her pots and pans around. It all happens right in front of her but she acts as if there's nothing going on. Her eyes don't see anything, her ears don't hear anything. Olivia, I start saying to myself, Olivia, maybe you're losing the plot. There's nothing going on in that kitchen. You've fried your brain and now you're seeing things. One thing's for sure, though, she told it to me herself, a long time ago: the four years he spent in prison were for procuring minors. He must have done some sick things. You don't get four years for nothing, do you? I reminded her of it and she screamed, "That doesn't mean anything, it was before we got married. Is that all you ever think about? God, you really are twisted."

'Why doesn't she look after her daughter? She knows what can happen. Granddad definitely raped her when she was little. It's as though people never learn anything from their lives . . . My mother, my sister and I, my other sister as well, and now my niece. It can't just be coincidence . . . I've been thinking to myself that maybe child abuse really is genetic.'

She breaks off, puts her hands on her hips, and waits for a response. She's kindly passing the matter over to me. She knows how much I like action.

'What do you mean, genetic? What kind of rubbish is that?'

'What I'm really worried about is school. Sophie's so serious, so calm and hardworking, a real head of the class. And nicely dressed, my sister makes sure of that. And you know what's going to happen, don't you. He's going to smash her little world to pieces. She'll lose interest in school, and then she'll stop going. By the time he's finished with her, all she's going to be good for is the street.'

'Why don't you make an official complaint?'

'For Sophie's sake. I know what would happen if I did: the police would come round and question her. She'd act dumb. She's never going to accuse her father of anything. He doesn't force her, he doesn't hit her; she thinks that's the way life is. The police go away again and nothing changes. Except me – I get kicked out, no one else goes to that dump, the kids will be left all on their own and he can carry on doing what he wants with them.'

'You could inform on him anonymously.'

'Oh yeah, sure. He'd never guess who grassed him up . . .'

'Well, so what if he does? At least the kids would understand that their parents haven't got the right to do what they're doing. It strikes me that it would be better to cut off contact than give it your support . . .'

'Hang on a minute,' Olivia says. 'I'm going to tell you something. When I turned up at Yvette's, I was thirteen. I'll spare you the details, I'm just telling you so you understand . . . When he had finished, he passed me on to his friends. And did I go to the police? No way. God, you've got no idea. I was happy. I'd become his woman. I was corrupted. And then Corinne showed up at Yvette's. I've never told you about Corinne, I haven't had the chance. Corinne's my other sister. She told me, "He did the same thing to me as he's doing to you. You've got to get out of here. You can come and stay at my place." All the time she was talking, Yvette was shouting abuse at her: "Bitch, bitch . . ." What did I do? Did I leave? Oh no. I stayed, of course.

'I've never seen Corinne since. I rang her, once. She asked me one question: "Do you still see him?" I said yes. She slammed the phone down. So tell me, what good has it done me, her cutting off all contact? As long as I keep going to their house, I can watch, and listen. At least the kids know that, when the time comes, they'll be able to count on me.'

'Wait a second. This doesn't make sense. Why do you go and spend weekends with them? Why do you ask them to help you move house? Why did you invite them to your show?'

'Because they're my family. They're all I've got. That's what you seem to find hard to understand.'

I see the brother-in-law's face, sweating on my stairs, I see the silhouette of the sister, standing on my landing. Then I see the children, the timid little brown-haired girl in her navy-blue coat, the boy in a jacket, polite, slightly dazed.

'I'm glad I've talked to you about it,' Olivia adds, as she takes the ashtray into the kitchen. 'Sometimes I don't know what to think any more. I don't know what I've seen. I'm scared I'm going mad.'

She leaves to go to bed. I hold her back by her sleeve.

'Olivia, I haven't had time to tell you in person. Your show was good. I mean, your show was fantastic. You were fantastic.'

'Yes,' is all Olivia says.

She looks at me with quiet certainty. I am taken aback for a moment. I'm not used to so much serenity.

'You know that already, don't you?'

'Yes, but it's nice of you to tell me as well. I've found two other courses. A clowning course, at the same school, and a drama course. I'm not sure why but I think that acting could be useful for me. When I move, all these thoughts come into my head. Maybe it's wrong to think this kind of work is just physical. The body can't talk but maybe it remembers all the words that have been said to it. But you should know about that, shouldn't you, what with all those books you read.'

13

'Start again. I haven't a clue what happened after 1991. What were you exactly, a promotions assistant or a cleaner?'

Olivia dives into a thick bundle of loose sheets of paper. I take advantage of the diversion to make some notes.

'Let me have a look at my payslips. OK, in January 1991 I was an assistant at the record company in the mornings and a cleaner in a shop in the evenings.'

'What does that involve, being an assistant?'

'I was responsible for checking the stock levels in the hypermarkets, opening the post, taking orders for merchandise like posters and what have you.'

'Not so fast, let me type that up . . . Assistant isn't enough. We'll go into detail. A good CV is very specific. And we'll leave out "cleaner", it's confusing.'

'Whatever you like.'

When Olivia asked me if I would type up her CV, I thought that it would only take a quarter of an hour. But the morning's nearly over. Soon we'll have been at it for two hours, and there're still three more years of her life left to type.

'It seems like you've done every job going.'

'Yes, but none of them for very long.'

'Don't worry, we can fudge it. We'll only put the best jobs in, and adjust how long you did them for.'

'Go ahead, you know better than me.'

'Alright, let's keep going. After promotions assistant . . .'

'Switchboard operator-stroke-accountant at the recording studio.'

'Accountant?'

Olivia giggles into her folder.

'I counted out the deals. And they went bankrupt. Put "switchboard operator", that'll do.'

Olivia is looking for a part-time job in the mornings. She'll carry on minding the children after school.

She has bought the newspapers and gone through the small ads. She has looked at the situations vacant at Franprix. She's been to the job centre. She's been to McDonald's. Disney. The town hall. She tells me, 'I'm the dregs of society. No bac, I haven't even studied up to baccalaureate level. I've got three choices as far as they're concerned: homelessness, prostitution or an overdose. The overdose would suit them best. I'm sick of this. I'm going to start asking people I know if they've got anything.'

She worries me. I'm not keen for her to start doing the recording studio's accounts again.

'You don't need to do just any old job. Not this year. I'm earning enough for us all at the moment.'

'I know. But I need money for my courses. By the way, can you lend me some cash to pay for my enrolment? If you can't, it doesn't matter, I'll manage. But I thought I'd rather ask you first. I hope you don't mind.'

I rummage around in the drawer of my desk, take out some of the money I got from the politician's book, and hand it over to Olivia with the solemnity of a graduation ceremony.

'Here you are.'

She could still refuse me. She could be a smart-arse. She might decide that she'd prefer to beg from who knows who, in exchange for who knows what. In the school of money she's a completely hopeless student. False alarm. She takes the money. She puts it in her pocket.

'You know you'll get it back,' she says.

'No rush.'

A friend of hers I've never met finds her a part-time job. Nine till two. Switchboard and cuttings on a weekly paper.

The paper is everything she could wish for. It's full of articles about TV celebrities. She knows all the people who work there personally, even the boss. She calls everybody *tu*.

She brings the latest issue back to the flat. I flick through it and throw it away. I don't want the children to find it. That rag degrades everything it touches, even the money needed to buy it.

'It's really cool,' Olivia explains, proud to be attending editorial meetings.

'Well I'm not cool. Not if it means being a total arsehole.'

Olivia doesn't take offence.

'I thought you wouldn't like it,' she says with satisfaction.

She's reassured. She never stops mapping my boundaries. She doesn't understand their coherence. I have to confirm and reconfirm them for her constantly. No, Olivia, no threesomes. No, no pornographic books. No, no videos either. No, no degrading newspapers. *No.*

'Ah,' she says, delighted, 'you don't like it . . . I knew you wouldn't.'

From then on, she leaves the paper at the switchboard.

✼

Olivia is waving an old copy of *Libération* which she found lying around in the bathroom.

'I know her!' she says victoriously.

She points to a photograph on the damp crinkled paper of a well-known film director, whose work is open, feminist and pro-vegetarian.

'She and my sister were in the same class at school. They're still friends.'

'Her? She's a friend of your sister's?'

'Yeah, you bet. She's very middle class, my sister. She's got a big house. She's a good host.'

I have trouble believing this. I can't picture how there could be any camaraderie between the unhinged Yvette and a feminist film director.

'They live in the same suburb, so they've stayed in touch. They have coffee together. She's really nice. Have you seen her films?'

One afternoon I come home unexpectedly. I can hear laughter, and talking, as I put down my bag. Olivia is entertaining friends. I take off my jacket and go into the living room.

Sitting on my chairs, around my table, are Olivia, a couple of students off her drama course, Yvette and the brother-in-law.

Olivia is holding forth. Her cheeks are flushed and she has a cigarette in her hand. She's sitting next to her brother-in-law, perched lopsidedly on one buttock, and leaning towards him. He has his arms crossed on the table. She's in the middle of telling a joke. I catch a bit of it. The joke is about condoms.

I don't say hello.

'Olivia, will you come and have a look at something for me, for a minute.'

She gets up, stubs out her cigarette and follows me.

We stand in the passage. She looks fixedly at me, arms dangling, an idiotic smile on her face. I speak slowly, in a low voice. I stress every syllable.

'I am going to buy some bread. I'll be gone for five minutes. You can deal with it however you like, but when I come back, I want them out of here. If they haven't left, I'll chuck you out with them. I forbid you to have them round here.'

I pick up my jacket and my bag and slam the door.

When I return, the gathering has melted away. Olivia is sluicing the cups out under a jet of water.

'How could you, Olivia? I mean, how *could* you?'

She bends over the sink. She doesn't answer. Barely ten minutes ago, she was laughing, talking about condoms and telling jokes. The brother-in-law was having a great time, with his arms folded. I wonder how far I should accept what I don't understand.

Sometimes when Olivia talks about her niece, she seems like a defeated army, a conquered soldier. Her eyes fill with tears of humiliation.

'He watches porn videos with her. My sister goes up to bed and he parks himself on the sofa with Sophie. The telly is right in the middle of the living room. How does my sister manage it? Does she block her ears? Don't you think he's a bastard? Do you think she really doesn't know what's going on? I can understand when it was me, I'm only her half-sister. But when it's her ten-year-old daughter, why doesn't she say anything?'

She repeats the same questions endlessly. She can't find any answers. As soon as she settles on one she spins off again.

Other times when she talks about it she sounds almost chatty. She tells me an anecdote and waits for my comments.

'Hey, my brother-in-law has come up with something new. Now his son's old enough to have girlfriends, he makes videos with the little girls.'

'With his son too?'

'Yes. He's showed me some of them. It's disgusting.'

'Hold on a minute. You watched them as well?'

'Yes. I had to see.'

'You watched them with the children?'

'Yes, at least then I know what's going on.'

'Christ, have you gone completely mad?'

'You think I shouldn't have watched them?'

'For fuck's sake, Olivia! It's not that you shouldn't have watched them. You shouldn't have allowed him even to talk to you about it.'

'But why?'

'Because it's evil! Don't you get it? It's *evil*.'

'Yes,' she says. 'That's what I thought. It is, isn't it?'

Sometimes she doesn't tell me anything; instead, I watch her pacing up and down in agitation, wringing her hands.

I repeat the same things to her endlessly, to reassure her. She never hears. I speak calmly. I'm often busy doing something else, working or reading with music on. The words come automatically, I never have to change them. She only listens to the music.

'Stop going on and on about him being a bastard. He's a criminal. You can take him to court and get him sent back to prison for twenty years. Society punishes child-abusers, it locks them up.'

'Yes,' she says. 'Yes.'

She paces up and down, thinking. 'I can't hate him. And that's what kills me.'

14

'But I thought you liked your job?'

We took the Metro to work together this morning. The carriages were packed with sad, tired people at that hour of day. We got squashed against the sliding doors.

At the stop for Saint-Ambroise, Olivia sighed. At Oberkampf, she wiped her eyes. At République, she burst into tears. I took her by the arm and led her out of the crowd.

'Come on, we'll go and have some coffee.'

We walked back up rue du Faubourg-du-Temple. Now she is sobbing into her cup.

'I don't want to go there any more,' she gulps, 'never again. And now I've made you late for your meeting . . . it's all my fault . . .'

She sniffs, and sucks a sugar lump. I haven't the heart to send her to work.

'You are going to go back home now and have a rest and then tomorrow we'll write your resignation letter. Don't look like that, at least you've earned a bit of money, it's not that bad. You'll soon find another job and they'll take on another switchboard operator.'

'Yes,' says Olivia.

But she doesn't go back to the flat. She dries her tears and goes in to the newspaper. In the evening, she no longer wants to resign.

Two days later she is sitting on the sofa, biting her nails. She is carefully dressed and made-up. Her eyelids look like mirages. She's waiting for a call. The call doesn't come.

I've set the computer up on the table so I can do some work. Or at least try to do some work while Olivia sighs behind me. I get exasperated.

'What's up this time?'

'Gérard asked me out to dinner and he was meant to ring me at nine o'clock. It's nearly ten and he still hasn't called.'

'Who's Gérard?'

'Gérard from the paper. He's the financial director, but he's in charge of personnel as well. He can't usually see me outside work because he's married, but he promised that he'd make up some story so we could go out this evening.'

'How old is he?'

'Forty. Fifty. Thirty-five. I don't know.'

Gérard was clearly a fast learner. I know the screenplay of his schooling off by heart and I've got the rushes in stock. I just need to splice them together.

So: Olivia arrives at the newspaper. She's very young, and pretty, and bright-eyed, she knows some good jokes about condoms. She's bubbly and good fun. She waits to see who will fall. It's Gérard! Bravo Gérard!

The switchboard is next door to his office, which is handy for the practical side of the operation.

He doesn't need anyone to spell out who he's dealing with. He knows her type. As things go on, she discovers fine qualities in his character, she decides he's nice. She's not hoping for anything specific, or at least nothing much more specific than a clandestine invitation to dinner. But there you go, this dinner would've been something like a decoration for her services to education, a form of recognition, a homage.

'But what did you think would happen? Did you really think he was going to complicate his life just because he's been carrying on with the switchboard operator in his office every morning?'

Yes, that was what she thought. She can't help it, she's always fucking up. Her make-up runs, the mirages trickle onto her cheeks. To console her, I'm forced to grant an amnesty to Gérard.

'Don't get into such a state. I'm not criticizing him. I'm more than happy to believe that he's nice. But you must have suspected that it wasn't serious . . .'

'I'm a shit,' Olivia groans, 'I'm a shit, I'm a shit.'

'Why are you crying? Are you in love with him?'

The tears stop. Her face brightens.

'No.'

'Have you ever been in love before?'

'No. Never.'

'Do you think you could fall in love one day?'

'No, never. I don't care, either. What I'd like would be to have a proper job, one which was useful to people, where I'd be loved and which I could be proud of.'

I suddenly come up with the explanation for Olivia's beatific smile, her over-generous heart. She is a nun. A primitive kind of nun, but a nun all the same.

Her heart is unable to enter into selfish unions. She gives all the love she has to us. To me, to the children, to her niece and nephew, to Amélie, and to the first no hoper she meets, to whom she will give her room and 800 francs.

She pardons the wicked, she calls them nice. She neither judges nor sentences her executioners. There is no room for hatred in her soul.

This charm which radiates from her and gives us warmth is the great goodness of lunatics and mystics. She has the dedication of the nun. The joy. The confusion. The lack of discernment. The kiss for the leper. The most sorely tested among us attain sainthood, provided they don't topple over into madness or crime. I'm living with a saint.

*

While I'm meditating on the human condition, Olivia is wondering, 'When you're in love, do you get jealous?'

'It seems to me yes, always a little.'

'You see . . . I never get jealous, I don't even know what it feels like. Even when things are going well with a man, I like him to have something going on on the side. It suits me that way. I just like to stay beside him, so I don't have to sleep on my own. I'll do the other stuff if he insists, but because of the way I feel about it, I'm hardly going to blame him if he needs to get his rocks off somewhere else.'

Olivia makes no secret of consenting readily to other people's desires. Sometimes she'll recall a rapid seduction in the middle of a story about something else. She takes a sardonic pride in it. If I didn't know her, I'd just think she was up for a good time. And fine about sex.

'But don't you like it at all?'

'That? No, no way. It doesn't do anything for me. Whenever I go out to a party with my friends, I always have to get out of my head first.'

'What friends?'

'Xavier, Benoît, all that lot.'

'Where did you meet them?'

'Oh, different places. Xavier works on a paper. Benoît is a film producer. They're who I see when I go out at night.'

'Oh right,' I say. 'I was wondering what on earth you were up to shooting off in the middle of the night like that, all done up like a Christmas tree. So, you go to parties?'

Olivia is a little agitated. She stubs out her cigarette and does up the laces of her boots for a second time.

'Alright, I'll tell you. I knew I'd end up telling you sooner or later. We go to Fred and Manu's, or Claude's, you know the sort of thing.'

'No, not really.'

Olivia looks at me critically.

'Oh, come on, Fred and Manu – you know, they have those parties, sex parties . . . At first, it's nice, we have a few drinks. But afterwards, it all gets complicated. I mean, I never refuse. But I can't do anything unless I'm completely out of it.'

'What about the state you're in when you get back in the morning? Are you seriously telling me that you all have a good laugh?'

'Yeah, I can't help it, at the time I feel fine. They're great, Xavier and Benoît. They ask me out, buy me drinks, let me sleep at their places afterwards. And you'll never guess all the famous people I've seen. Go on, say some names . . . Film stars, comedians, TV presenters. Still, you know, it's like anywhere else, you meet some total jerks. But some of the people are really nice, as well, I promise you.'

'Oh, come on, stupid, when are you going to learn? What, some-one's just got to give you a packet of sweeties to make you drop your pants and then you cry your eyes out about it afterwards? And all you can say is that it's *funny*?'

'Don't get mad at me. It was the same when I was a kid. You should have seen my brother-in-law, he'd take me out in his van and the whole lot of them would give me a going over in the back. The guys would be laughing, I couldn't see anything wrong with it, I thought we were friends. Though when I left that house, I was a complete alcoholic. I'm not saying it's my brother-in-law's fault, after all, my mother was an alcoholic. But still, not everybody's an alcoholic at fifteen.'

Gérard never came to take Olivia out to dinner. Next day she asks me to help her write her letter of resignation.

Gérard calls her into his office. He gives her back her letter and offers her redundancy instead. He adds a month's pay in lieu of notice and 2,000 francs in cash. She's found the money for the courses. One morning she calls at the flat. She takes a bundle of notes out of her pocket and carefully unfolds it.

'This is for you,' she says.

She pays me back, in fifties.

'Just now, on the boulevard,' Olivia tells me, 'I bumped into a guy I met at one of the parties. I said hello. I thought he was going to stop and shake my hand, maybe ask me to have a cup of coffee with him. But no, he scuttled off like a rat. At first I thought he didn't recognize me. But then I realized that he had done it on purpose. Don't you think someone who does that is a real bastard? He could at least have said hello to me, don't you think?'

15

We spend the nights talking, I study the passing icebergs, and life goes on. We have started reading *Huckleberry Finn* out loud. Laurent is depressed and I go and have coffee with him in the mornings. I find his depressions comforting. My parents don't ring – I assume they're happy; no news is good news. The Monopoly set gathers dust on top of the children's wardrobe, having been usurped by something called 'The Good Wage' which consists of managing a family budget: taxes, loans, sundry expenses and maintenance. Winning the Lottery is allowed.

I stop smoking. I stop drinking. I believe in God. I become a vegetarian. None of it lasts for more than six hours. I am often disheartened.

*

Denis comes back from Canada. He drops by one evening, without warning, when I've got guests. Exhausted from the journey, he greets everybody distractedly, then goes straight to my room, gets into my bed and falls asleep. Laurent is filled with admiration for such off-handedness.

'All photographers are sex addicts,' he announces with triumphant self-assurance. 'Who can blame them – after all, looking is their job.'

Denis gets up before morning and goes back to his own flat.

I look at the posters for magazines stuck up in newsagents' windows. They're next to the adverts for chatlines. The girls are all young. They show their breasts, their tongues, they spread their thighs, they offer up their backsides.

I no longer see the breasts; all I see is the faces. I wonder to myself. Where does this one come from? Was she in care? Maybe she's Russian? What brought her to posing for this photo? How much did she get paid for it? And what does she do with the money she's earned?

'Feminists are whores,' exclaims Laurent, one evening when I've got some people round for dinner.

He's a bit drunk. He loves an ideological debate.

'They dream of cutting our balls off. Have you read about the inquisition that's terrorizing campuses in America? Imagine a professor in France being hounded because he flirted with a student . . .'

His current sweetheart settled at his side exudes approval. She's hypnotized. She looks adoringly at him. She chants: Feminists are whores, feminists are whores.

Laurent sings the praises of a friend of his, a philosophy tutor, a bit of an artist as well, who privately prides himself on giving a few extra marks to the students he thinks are pretty. And then asking them out to dinner. Laurent is ecstatic. Those misappropriated marks are

Laurent's crowning glory, his 1789, his 1792. He loves a victorious leader: Mitterrand, de Gaulle, Napoleon.

He's still holding forth when I clear away the plates and bring in the pudding. I ignore his provocation. He's not going to draw me into this idiotic argument.

'When I think about poor Woody Allen, and the conspiracy that bitch Mia Farrow started about him, I wonder what the world's coming to.'

He sneaks a look at me out of the corner of his eye.

'Hey, stupid,' I say, my hands full of plates, 'you're starting to get on my nerves. If poor old Woody wants conjugal bliss, all he has to do is avoid incest.'

'What do you mean, incest?'

Laurent smirks at me with satisfaction. I've entered his net. He can't wait to pull the cord tight. In a few minutes, I'll have had it.

'Just what I said, incest.'

'Oh bullshit. The girl's adopted.'

'Exactly. Adoption makes it worse. According to the anthropologist Françoise Héritier, who is one of the leading authorities on kinship.'

Laurent laughs a mocking laugh. He calls the gathering to witness.

'That's ideological force-feeding. The only reason the feminist rabble wants his head is because the girl's young. Which is what's known as a sectional claim, you poor dupe. No one's ever going to stop me thinking it's great when a sixty-year-old guy manages to walk off with a young girl. That'll teach the old bag a lesson!'

The men around the table laugh. They watch me. They appraise my figure under my shirt.

'And anyway,' Laurent continues, beaming, 'this Françoise Héritier of yours is a woman, am I right? Might we be allowed to know how old she is?'

I could throw him out. I hesitate for a second, but it's late and I haven't got the courage. I take refuge in the kitchen and wash up the plates. Next door they yell with joy and laugh about Farrow's big arse and her ridiculous hair. It's total uproar, I hope it doesn't wake the children. I should be proud: my dinner parties are a great success, the guests are witty. People always have a good time.

When the guests have gone I sink into my sofa, alone, and let the rage come over me. Things are usually easier. I'm used to confrontations with my brother. I know what the sex war is a cover for, between us: the fratricidal war. The two of us have no better or stronger bond than these confrontations and we are always renewing them.

Sometimes I take my revenge. I wave UN, UNICEF and ILO reports under his nose. I read out, in public, accounts of the torments inflicted on women, the unpunished crimes committed by his fellow men in China, in India, in Russia, in Afghanistan, in the Arab Emirates, in Serbia, in Thailand . . . I invoke the bodies of murdered little girls.

Laurent puts up a poor show of resistance. He can't keep it up for very long. He is like anybody else – he has his temperamental outbursts. He usually ends up ripping the file out of my hands. I don't care, I can talk without notes.

At last he cries, 'But it's not my fault!'

By that stage, I feel a little sorry for him. Fundamentally, he'd so much like to be a good person. But he exhausts me. So I finish him off. 'It is, it is your fault. You've never done anything except set up your tent with the executioners. What have you learnt from history to allow you to claim nothing's your fault?'

He leaves the room, beating a retreat. I put my piles of paper down on the table. I can't lose every battle.

Normally, I have no qualms about engaging in this rivalry. It's usually invigorating. So why, this evening, does it make me feel like crying?

I am worn out and fragile. I'm tired of confrontations. Just for a little while, I'd like it if desire could be an extinct volcano, and we were simply meadows on its fertile slopes.

16

I can't get Olivia's stories out of my head. The iceberg is wrecking my natural desire. My boundaries, my distinctions between the honest and the criminal are gradually being lost in a fog of confusion.

For a while now I have been an unenthusiastic participant in the love-making that was once my delight and my consolation. But I'm fading. My mind is full of filth. What distinguishes us from the Lerouillys or their neighbours or the Xaviers or the Benoîts? I'm floundering and sinking deeper. I'm furious. I didn't know until now that I was naked. But I have eaten from the tree of knowledge and I'm being punished: I am naked and I disgust myself.

One night after we've been to the cinema and we're drinking casually at his kitchen table, I ask Thierry to tell me one of the fantasies he keeps tucked away in the recesses of his desire. I keep on insisting. I wait. Finally he answers with a diffident smile. Well, he sometimes dreams about a very young girl. He says it innocently. He's repeating an old memory, almost apologetically. A very young girl who I seduce. There you go, not very original, is it?

And that's me well and truly caught, me and my stupid curiosity. It's my own fault, and here I am, once again stuck in the dark with my mental map up to my face, searching for the boundaries separating the good from the wicked. Looked at this way, it's not a question of images any more, or a question of desire; in fact, it's not a question of anything at all. I stretch out beside Thierry, turn my back on him and go to sleep with my face in the pillow.

Things are no simpler with Denis. He makes a passing observation about how he finds the mugginess of peep-shows moving, how strip-teases and bodies in windows make him nostalgic.

'You sound as if you're talking about things, but those are living people you're looking at and trading in,' I remind him.

'That's what makes it unsettling,' he replies, 'and so attractive. Do you think I'm a bastard?'

'Yes, of course,' I say, 'or no, I don't know. Why are you telling me all this? I'm starting to get sick of it. I'm not your mother.'

We're in the same deep water, Denis and I; sometimes it's clearer and sometimes more muddy. It's not so easy to establish boundaries in the water, it's mad how much time I spend putting out buoys.

I am growing in humanity. I don't know if I should thank Olivia for it, or curse her. But if things carry on like this, I wouldn't give much for my libido's chances.

However, I can't completely renounce the pleasures of love. I am going to have to come to some agreement with the world. I muster my resistance. I develop a new mental discipline and force myself to observe it.

I imagine a giant font, a sort of hip-bath, ribbed like a shell. I immerse myself in it and pray.

Lord, bless our beds.

Bless men, bless women and bless their bodies.

Bless blowjobs, bless long secret kisses, and the different caresses and cries that accompany them.

Bless our imaginations, our dreams and our nightmares.

And Lord, bless sodomy.

But deliver us from evil, and deliver our children from evil.

Forgive us our trespasses.

And destroy the wicked.

I return home from the cinema with Cécile. It's very late but I ask her in for a cup of coffee anyway. Olivia is on the sofa watching TV, waiting for me. We've hardly got through the door before she leaps up. She has her warpaint on, and her coat.

'Oh, Olivia, are you sure?' is all I say.

'Yes,' she replies, heading for the door. 'See you tomorrow.'

I accompany her to the door and shut it gently behind her.

'What's up?' asks Cécile.

'Oh nothing,' I say. 'A sort of routine.'

The next day, I find Olivia in the kitchen looking pale and drinking her coffee in silence. I don't hang around. I take my cup and go back to my room. She's the one who follows me.

'I'd like to stop but I can't help myself,' she begins, even though I haven't said anything to her.

'You've got other friends. You could go and stay over at their places when you want to go out. Agnès, Armelle, Jean-Luc – that lot – they're always pleased to see you.'

'I know,' says Olivia, with a discouraged smile. 'But it's not the same.'

'Exactly,' I say.

'Exactly,' she repeats.

She gets bored with them – with their books, with their great kindness and faultless generosity. She's bored the whole time. She has to make such an effort to listen to what they're saying and answer them intelligently: such an effort to deserve their attention and their respect.

It's fine seeing them now and then, but not too often, no, she's young, she wants to go out. She wants to have fun.

'Do you get bored with me as well?' I ask her.

One day Olivia clears out my cupboards. She makes a heap of all the clothes I never wear and stuffs them into a binbag. She forces me to agree to her plan before trying to close it. She swings it over her shoulder. She's going to take it to Chiffoniers d'Emmaüs, the charity shop at the end of the avenue. She asks me to sort out my library so she can give some books to a hostel for young girls in the 11th arrondissement.

'It drives me mad,' she says, 'all these things people have in their houses which they don't use.'

She knows all the children at the kids' school and the parents as well. She is up to date with everyone's worries – the Peruvian grandparents who can't get a visa, the kids who never have breakfast, the mothers who have to work so much that they're late collecting their children. Some she sympathizes with, some she stuffs with biscuits. She introduces the overwhelmed mothers to me and I invite their kids to sleep over. She has never been on a protest march in her life but she comes with me on a rally against the new immigration laws. She watches the meagre crowd scattered about the Place de la Nation with amazement and scepticism. She doesn't stay long.

'I've only come for little Paula's sake,' she says, 'she needs her grandparents.'

Thanks to Olivia, I understand that good is not the opposite of bad, day is not the opposite of night, white is not the opposite of black. It's more and less simple than that. Olivia's genius saunters through the territory of goodness, whistling.

THIRD PART

I

Agnès and I were lying side by side under the duvet, drinking verbena tea and watching the fire.

'What about Olivia, are things OK with her?' Agnès asked me.

'Yes,' I said noncommittally, stifling the urge to say more.

What I knew about Olivia had been uncommunicable for quite some time. Still, I would have liked to pass on some of the burden. To say to someone, 'You'll never guess what Olivia told me.'

'No . . .'

'Well . . .'

But the words always stopped there. I struggled to articulate them. Rapes, child abuse; sticks in her vagina. No really, what would be the good of uttering these words without a reason? I'm not a police-woman or a doctor or a lawyer. There would have been an idiotic brutality in using them idly, a brutality towards me, towards Olivia and towards whoever was called upon to listen to them.

Sometimes I carried on regardless and immediately regretted it.

For example, I once told someone, 'Olivia was raped when she was little.'

'Oh, really! That's no great surprise!' the person I was talking to had responded angrily, and I had fallen silent.

But equally, if they had insisted with unabashed curiosity, 'No way! Tell me!', I would have clammed up as well, horrified by their desire to hear more and not wanting to gratify it.

Besides, where and when would I have had the opportunity to unload my little dump-truck? In my parents' kitchen at the end of a boozy lunch? At a friend's flat, on somebody's birthday? In the evening, on the Metro, as I chatted to a colleague who took the same line as me?

I knew that, in the telling, the only thing left would be anecdotes, the bare bones of the story which have no meaning. There'd be noth-ing of the evenings we'd spent together laughing with the children, nothing of what drives us, the troubles we share, of our affection, or of our reason. These stories are always the same, you don't have to go far to find a thousand others like it. The papers are full of them, our families are full of them – packed with children who've been deceived and young people who want to die. Anybody who doesn't know one of these stories first hand must have been walking around with their eyes shut.

So I didn't talk about Olivia to Agnès. She hated sad, complicated stories, anyway. She preferred to master her grief. She'd climb on her motorbike and speed round the *périphérique*. 'It calms me down,' she'd growl, 'it calms me down.' Sometimes I'd get on the bike behind her and loop my arms around her waist, resting my cheek on the cold leather of her jacket.

The windows of the flat were open to the full expanse of the sky, and torrents of light were flooding in. Agnès had just left, and I was drinking cold coffee on my own.

The three of them crept up behind me in their pyjamas.

'We've got something to tell you,' Olivia announced at the top of her voice.

Thomas and Suzanne were jumping about.

'Happy Birthday! Go on, Suzanne, give it to her.'

Suzanne stretched out her arms. Resting on her open palms was a little rectangular package tied up with a proper royal-blue ribbon.

I undid the ribbon. Under the paper, a box. In the box, a pen. A ballpoint, Veronese green body, slender but heavy, with a gilt band round its middle. You had to twist it to make the tip come out.

'I've never had such a lovely pen,' I declared. 'And it's just right for my work as well! I'm going to use it all the time.'

'You see! I told you,' Olivia murmured in Thomas's ear.

I was fervently admiring my present when Olivia took it out of my hands.

'This pen you see here,' she declared solemnly, 'is guaranteed for life.'

'For life,' Thomas repeated.

A gust of pride blew through the room, ruffling our hair as it passed. I felt suddenly mortal. Or immortal. Or maybe it was the pen that was immortal. Or mortal. It was all a bit confused, but nevertheless, in the meantime we were dry and warm and up there on the summit of Olympus.

I thanked Olivia in the passage.

'It's a really beautiful present. I know you bought it, thank you.'

Olivia nodded her head affably.

'It's normal, isn't it. You've got to celebrate birthdays, for the children's sake. For our sakes too, mind you. We're not animals.'

2

The streets and squares were heavy with the smell of hyacinths and rain that comes with spring, that scent that's so affecting in the city where it blends with the dust thrown up by diesel lorries and the petrol fumes. Where does it come from, this hyacinth smell? Probably from our memory of the seasons, and our longing for them. Autumn has its own scent – of apples, fog and damp wood. Winter smells of smoke, summer of vanilla. And it is by no means the least miracle of cities that they remind us of how blue hyacinths are, even though we never see them – strangers to our physical surroundings but not to our manipulative desires.

Well anyway, it was spring, the season that makes the sap rise in women so that they grow pretty and cheerful. I should have joined in the general awakening as well, but I couldn't seem to. With each new day I grew a little sadder.

It wasn't that I was entirely without joy, or lamenting its absence; courage was what was failing me, courage and strength.

In the evening, I'd sometimes fall asleep in the middle of reading *Treasure Island* to the children. My eyes would sting, the lines would start to overlap on the page, I'd hear my voice beginning to falter, and then my head would slip onto my shoulder and I'd doze off. Suzanne and Thomas would abandon me on the sofa without holding it against me. Olivia would put them to bed in their room, then silently go upstairs. I'd wake up on my own in the dark. Sometimes I'd work, sometimes I'd go to bed.

I kept having dreams in which I discovered secret rooms in my flat. Sometimes the rooms opened onto gardens that had been left to run wild. Or I'd move into menacing buildings with high ceilings and tall stained-glass windows. My children and I would be forced to sleep in the doorways, it was always the wrong house, I was incapable of settling down.

Fatigue overcame me completely. Nothing withstood it any more – neither coffee nor love nor alcohol. I tried to resist, I pushed my body to the limit. But the more I tried to ignore it, the more it took me over. I no longer had a mind or a spirit, I was reduced to this burdensome, sad body which spent a lot of its time crying. What an awful spring, when I think about it now, God, what an awful spring.

Logically, or at least according to what served as logic for me, there came a time when I began to think about dying. I couldn't see any other way out of my exhaustion. When I thought about the world, it seemed a more harmonious place without me. The idea felt familiar and I carried it round with me all day long, without fear or anger, I thought – I who was eaten up with fear and anger.

I found the idea of death reassuring and painless compared to everything else: the exhausted mornings, the rent to pay, the articles to hand in and Mylène, who summoned me to interminable rewriting meetings where she'd browbeat me like a naughty child who's been pulling the wings off flies. I had to swear that I liked the work she gave me and I'd say yes yes yes, telling myself that I could always die if I wanted, I wasn't a prisoner, of anything or anyone, I could walk out on them all, soon, at least where I'd be going there wouldn't be anyone to give me a hard time.

I was making plans for the future. I relied on Jean-Patrick to look after the children when I wasn't around any more. I trusted him very much, he was so tenderly paternal. I had no doubt that he would remarry in a flash. He'd know how to choose a friendly, conscientious wife.

At this stage of my thinking, I'd inevitably burst into tears. I loved Thomas and Suzanne too much to give up their company, the bond joining me to them was so strong that it lashed me down, in spite of myself, to everything I no longer wanted.

But as the days passed, I began to doubt more and more seriously what I could possibly give my children. I was falling into a deep well, whose sides were made of doubts and constraints. I was falling alone and endlessly.

One Friday I resolved to die. I called Jean-Patrick and asked him if he could take the children even though it wasn't his weekend. Just this once. I said that I had work that was taking up too much time and reports that were late to finish. I invoked our shared need of money.

Jean-Patrick agreed without hesitation.

'Are you tired?'

'Yes, I'm wiped out actually.'

'I know what you mean,' said Jean-Patrick. 'I've asked to go part time, I really need to write and do some sport. That's the advantage of the public sector; you don't earn much but you do have a bit of time. I'll pick up the kids on Saturday morning.'

In the evening I didn't bother to do any work. What's the point of working when you're going to die the next day?

I was on my own. Olivia had gone out without telling me where she was going, which suggested that she wouldn't be back for a while. I sat down with a bottle of vodka and watched TV all evening, waiting for the morning. I had no memories, no plans, nothing left except waiting and resolve. Jean-Patrick would come and get the children and then I'd be alone and undisturbed.

But that evening Olivia had simply gone to the cinema. After the film, she came by the flat before going up to her room.

It was pretty late when she came into the living room. I didn't hear her key in the lock. I just raised my eyes from the TV at one point and she was there, looking at me in consternation.

'Hey,' I mumbled, 'you're here.'

She didn't say anything. Without taking off her jacket, she switched off the telly and took the bottle of vodka into the kitchen. I thought for a second that she wanted to talk to me, but no, to my momentary amazement she didn't try to start a conversation. As for me, I didn't feel up to starting to talk first; the words would have stuck in my mouth. I could feel them forming a thick paste; they wouldn't have got past my tongue. I was in two minds about standing up. I felt a little nauseous. I didn't move or speak and waited for her to go up to bed, hoping my silence would discourage her. It was a waste of effort. She took off her jacket and threw it on a chair.

'Go and get into bed,' she said. 'I'm going to sleep in the living room.'

She was giving me an order, a solid, straightforward order, for me to prop myself up against. What a nerve. I was too drunk to complain. I did as she said and slowly stood up from the sofa. Olivia took a T-shirt out of the ironing basket and threw a blanket over the sofa.

'Are the children here?'

'They're asleep.'

I walked across the room, annoyed. Then I wanted to turn off the light.

'Leave it,' she said. 'You know I can't sleep in the dark.'

She tuned the radio to NRJ, turned up the volume and wrapped herself in the blanket.

I fell on my bed without taking off my clothes and turned off the lamp. I didn't think I'd be able to get to sleep, the alcohol was turning my stomach. But from my darkened room I could see the living-room light shining in the passage and hear the monotonous drone of the radio, so I cried and fell asleep.

It was the morning. From time to time I'd open my eyes and hear Olivia, Thomas and Suzanne talking in the kitchen. They chattered away, getting the things they needed for the weekend ready – a game, a doll, some socks which they stuffed in a bag. I closed my eyes, and a stream of images, like patterns on fabric, passed behind my eyelids: bowls, palm trees, plump cherries, naively-rendered waterfalls. A little later I heard Olivia discouraging Jean-Patrick from coming and saying hello to me.

'Leave it for now. She worked very late last night, she needs to rest. She'll call you at home later . . .'

Soon they left, my children and their father, who seemed so joyful to me and so fit to live. I was all used up.

On the top shelf of the bathroom cupboard I had accumulated enough pills to put me to sleep for good. Provided, of course, that I was left alone long enough to die. Provided Olivia vacated the premises.

But she was doing something in the kitchen. Then in the children's room. Then in the living room. Then she was ironing in front of the telly – I could hear the dreary commentary of a wildlife documentary punctuated by damp belches from the iron.

What was she up to? Why didn't she clear off and get on with her business – her good works, her friends, her acting – as she normally did on a Saturday? Why didn't she have an appointment with the gynaecologist, the vascular specialist, the psychotherapist?

I got up and ran to the kitchen to make a last cup of coffee. I'm only human. The flat smelled to high heaven of toast.

'Hello,' Olivia called out as I went down the passage.

She abandoned her ironing and followed me into the kitchen.

'Sit down, I'll make it for you.'

She didn't ask me about my physical health or my mental health. In fact, she didn't even look at me. She made me some coffee and some toast, plastering it with a thick layer of butter.

'Haven't you got anything to do today?' I asked after my first cup of coffee.

My head was pounding. I screwed up my eyes as I spoke, the sound of my voice made me wince.

'I don't know yet. It depends. I'll see,' she replied laconically, obviously keen to avoid giving me any guarantees.

'But I've got to work,' I insisted, closing my eyes, 'I need some peace and quiet.'

'Yes, yes.'

With that, she refilled my cup and went and locked herself in the bathroom.

She stayed there for a long time. I went back to bed and became lost in thought. I mean, I cried hot tears, giving up on all engagement with the world and abandoning myself to despair.

By the time she came out of the bathroom, my eyes were stinging. She came into my room and contemplated my bed. I was rolled up in a ball under the duvet, hiding my ravaged face.

'Come out of there,' she said, 'I know things aren't alright, but there's no need to go over the top.'

I poked my nose out of my cotton burrow.

'If you could only see your face, it's almost funny. I've run you a bath, you should go and get into it.'

She sat down on the edge of the bed, wrapped in a bath towel. Her hair was tied up on her head oddly, in a sort of topknot with the ends hanging down over her face.

'Olivia, I'm losing it,' I said.

'If you want to know what I think,' she said, picking up a packet of cigarettes off my desk, 'you've been losing it for quite a while.'

And she lit a cigarette.

'You should go and have a bath. It'll do you good.'

I went to the bathroom. I didn't want to have a bath. I wanted to look at my trusty store of pills on the top of the cupboard. I raised myself on tiptoe, pushed aside the stacks of towels and slapped the furthest corners of the shelf with my hand. There was nothing there. Not one of the packets which I'd so carefully collected and hidden out of sight. Not a single one. Distraught, I got undressed and slid into the caressing water. The bath was so full that the smallest movement would have caused a tidal wave. For a long time I looked at my legs, distorted through the water. I was amazed by my feet, by the pattern of little bones and veins stretched taut under the delicate skin, my minutely detailed feet with all their toes in the right place. The steamy heat went to my head and I nearly dropped off.

By mid-morning I was clean and dressed and breakfasted and the first hours of this day of mourning had begun to seem like a hangover. I felt ridiculous, ridiculous and pathetic.

'Olivia,' I said.

She'd set about tidying my room and was stacking my papers in symmetrical piles on my desk, with complete disregard for their content.

'Where are the pills which were on the top shelf of the bathroom cupboard?'

'Haven't a clue,' Olivia said, raising her eyes to the ceiling. 'Do you expect me to keep track of everything in this flat? Maybe I took them when I wasn't well . . .'

'Don't talk rubbish. You've taken them away, haven't you?'

'No.'

'Yes you have.'

'Prove it.'

She stared at me insolently. If it hadn't been for my conspicuous distress, she would have laughed in my face.

'I want a pill for this morning,' I negotiated.

'OK, just for this morning. Afterwards you'll have to ask for them.'

I sat down on my bed and started crying again.

'Oh dear,' she said. 'Don't move, I'll go and find you something.'

She gave me two Lysanxia and I went back to bed.

3

No matter that it had been an awful spring; that suicidal Saturday was a good Saturday, a Saturday of great rest and peaceful solitude.

As I'd been intending to abandon the world, I hadn't planned any activities. After all I was between life and death. I could stay in bed for as long as I wanted. The telephone rang, but Olivia fielded the calls. I was in no-man's-land, presumed dead, I was a sick child who's allowed to skip their homework, a child wracked by feverish dreams.

The terrible anguish, the one that stops you from sleeping and forces you to take action, went away in the end. Olivia came into my room at regular intervals and stuck one or two bluish pills in my mouth, which instantly sent me back to the meadows of sleep. On the dot of four, she even offered me a glass of vodka, on the old-fashioned pretext that it was a 'hair of the dog'. By four thirty I was totally spaced out.

'Maybe you should take it easy now,' Olivia muttered when I tried to thank her with a sodden look in my eyes and a fixed smile. My words of thanks seemed to vanish as they came into contact with the air and I wasn't sure what I wanted to say to her any more. Intemperate tears rolled down my cheeks and I caught them on the tip of my tongue, which made me laugh like an idiot.

It was dark when she yelled in my ear, 'Wake up! It's time to eat.'

She pulled my duvet off me and dragged me into the living room. The television was on, throwing its loud, coloured light round the room. Sitting regally on the carpet was a flat, grey cardboard box.

'*Pizza la reine*, sixty-five francs, my treat,' she said, '*Bon appétit.*'

I sat down cross-legged. I had trouble eating in a dignified way. The pizza refused to remain in my slack mouth and pieces kept escaping and tumbling onto my knees. I picked them up and put them back in my mouth. Olivia didn't look at me, but fixed her gaze on the telly.

Then it was night. I know Olivia stayed in the living room and watched over my heavy sleep, but I don't remember a thing.

A new day began, there were croissants and coffee and another hot bath and Olivia still watching me without saying anything. I had a headache, I was empty and alive. Then the overpowering fear suddenly returned. I was going to have to start it all up again. Fill the fridge, get back on the Metro, answer the phone, pay the rent and finish the articles that were late. My pulse began throbbing all over my body. I put my hand to my chest and pressed on my heart to try and calm its agitation.

'Oh, shit,' I said.

'You can say that again,' agreed Olivia. 'You're going to have to give me a bit of a hand otherwise I'll never be able to cope. Here, have half a pill. I'm not going to give you any more for the moment, I don't want you dying on me.'

I went back to bed and Olivia decided to put my library in order. I thought it was a pretty funny idea for her to come up with, seeing as she couldn't care less about books. She planted herself in the passage in front of the bookshelves and shouted out questions to me. I replied from under my duvet.

'Hey, how about I arrange them by size and colour? That would be less ugly, for a start.'

'No, that's not the right way to do it.'

'OK then, I'll read out the titles and you can tell me where they should go.'

'No, that'll never work, I have to think how to classify them . . .'

'God, what a fuss! Here I am, offering to tidy up, and all you can say is that it's impossible! I swear, it's like coming back to a pigsty, this flat, all these books piled up any old how, it's like you don't give a shit. If you'd sorted them out then you could give me some for the library at the hostel. You're not going to tell me you need to keep them all. OK, I'm going to start with this one, *Les Pensées*, you've got three copies, all by the same writer, it's probably the same book, in fact, it's as old as anything, why do you need three of them? Mind you, they're not going to want that sort of thing at the hostel, books that are old enough to have grandchildren, who's going to be interested in *them*, I ask you . . . Right, I'll tell you the one next to it, *Les Amours*. Oh well, at least the girls will like that one, you should see how silly they are – and that's just the ones who can read . . . I'm going to make two piles . . . OK, I'm carrying on: *Les Essais*. Wow, this isn't a library, it's a dictionary!'

She was standing in the passage, yelling, and I could hear her hurling books onto the carpet. I couldn't stand it any longer. I jumped out of bed.

'Let me see.'

'Put the ones you really like to one side,' she suggested, kicking a wobbly pile of books out of her way, 'we'll sort them out first. Hey, *Les Misérables*, why does that ring a bell?'

'It's good, maybe you should try reading it . . .'

'Oh God, she's off again . . . I'm not your daughter!'

'How about if I mark the good bits?'

'We'll see, put it aside. But don't give me a lecture, this isn't the time. We're working.'

For two hours, we emptied the shelves. Our hands grew black and our noses were smudged with dust. I stroked the soft books as I took them down and noted the jagged edges of the pages that I'd slit in too much of a hurry, with a kitchen knife. From behind the shelves I recovered a picture book illustrating the seasons which had belonged to my grandfather. I found a long-lost envelope full of large square negatives which my grandmother had given me to develop for her, when I was a teenager. I'd never got them developed and now my grandmother was dead and I had become the guardian of faces to which I would never be able to put a name. I also found a poem of Suzanne's about birds and thunder, a very lovely poem. When I read it to Olivia she went into ecstasies.

'Chuck out the books and keep the poem,' she suggested.

It was a tempting suggestion, but a bit extreme. I declined, despite the respect I have for Suzanne.

Olivia was hungry. The books were sprawled at the foot of the shelves. I was incapable of deciding on a system of classification, and I knew we were going to end up putting them back on the shelves at random. I contemplated the shambles with my arms dangling, in that particular state of discouragement God must have felt on the morning of the seventh day when he turned round and was confronted with the anarchy of Creation.

'A pill?' Olivia suggested, in an appealing voice.

'No thanks, I think I'd rather have something to eat.'

'Fine, I'll clean this and you can cook us something. Have you seen my finger after I've run it across one of the shelves? Look at the colour of it! I need a bowl and the stepladder. You'll see, maybe they won't all be sorted out but at least they'll be clean.'

I opened the fridge. There wasn't much in there, but then you don't need much to cook for two – a lemon, an onion, some pasta shells. I cooked while she sprayed the white plastic-covered shelves with Ajax. She kept up a continuous flow of chatter. Now she was talking about Dr Cajoudiara.

'It wasn't really anything he said to me,' she bawled. 'When I remember things he said they're just small talk, really – it was more that he was good at talking. Oh, you would have loved him. You could tell him anything, he wasn't at all precious. "Olivia," he'd say to me, "Olivia, you'll see, in a few years . . ." Speaking of which, have you thought of going to see a psychiatrist yourself?'

I tried a pasta shell. It was translucent, with a sweet taste of onion. We were ready to eat when a dreadful crash ricocheted from the passage to the kitchen. I dropped my spoon and rushed out. Olivia was lying on the floor surrounded by scattered books. She had fallen off the stepladder, pulling down a whole row of plywood shelves in her fall.

'It's not serious,' she groaned. She was completely white. 'Your whole bloody library fell on my head, that's all.'

She grimaced as I gently lifted her up by the shoulders. I tried to set her on her feet, but she fell back with a cry.

'I think it's my ankle,' she whispered. 'I twisted my foot when I fell and now I've probably broken it. Talk about bad luck.'

'Emergency doctors? Are you crazy?' she protested from her cradle of paper, as I dialled the number. 'You know how useless they are! They'll say I've got a sore throat and I'll end up dying here like an idiot surrounded by all your books. Hang up! Now! We're going to casualty. Call a cab, hang on, I know the number off by heart . . .'

In the waiting room with her leg up on the back of a chair, she made lots of friends. She also hit it off with the young house doctor, a pleasant, redhaired guy who diagnosed a sprained ankle and bandaged her foot meticulously.

'If you want to get better, you mustn't move for a fortnight. Not move at all, do you understand?' he said with youthful assurance.

Olivia gave me a euphoric look.

'A fortnight!' she murmured. 'You're going to have to look after me for a fortnight.'

'At least that'll be a fortnight of you not going out at all hours with any passing halfwit and getting up to every stupid thing you can think of.'

'So? Aren't you pleased?'

'Yes, very. You'll have time to read *Les Misérables*.'

We had to stop the taxi outside a chemist's, then outside a grocer's so I could get some food for supper. Afternoon was shading into evening when we eventually got back to the flat.

I settled Olivia on the sofa and spread a blanket over her to keep her warm. The pasta shells lost their sweet scent when I reheated them. I filled two plates and took them in to the living room.

'Not bad,' concluded Olivia. 'Pity I emptied the rest of the vodka down the sink, there's nothing left to drink.'

I didn't make tea, because I knew she loathed it. I didn't go and exhume *Les Misérables* from the tumulus of abandoned books, either.

'I haven't got time to read it now,' said Olivia. 'I've got work to do for my drama course. We're going to put on *Les Précieuses Ridicules*, do you know it?'

'Yes.'

'I thought so. I nicked your copy. Don't worry, you'll get it back. I tried to read it, but I can't see what's supposed to be funny about it. This isn't a criticism, but do you honestly think that play makes people laugh?'

I went up to her room. Beside her bed, I picked up my ageless Larousse edition of *Les Précieuses Ridicules*. I brought down a few clothes, her toothbrush, an address book and the photo of her mother. I double-locked the door on my way out.

Then I sat down beside her with a tube of aspirin within reach and *Les Précieuses Ridicules* in my hand.

'Let's go,' I said, opening the book with relish.

'You're happy now, aren't you? At last you're going to get a chance to educate me.'

'I'm very happy. But I wonder if it was really necessary for you to break your foot first.'

'I didn't hurt my foot on purpose,' said Olivia. 'It ran away from me.'

4

'"Your fear outruns your injury, and your heart cries out before it is touched."'

'"The deuce it does! It is flayed from head to foot."'

'A heart flayed from head to foot . . . You can see that that's funny, can't you?'

'No.'

'Oh come on, for goodness sake make an effort, this is the funniest scene in the whole play.'

'There's no need to get cross. Maybe it is funny, it just doesn't make me laugh. It's no big deal.'

'It's my fault, I must have explained it badly. Let's start again.'

'What? From the *beginning*?'

'No, just this scene.'

'Oh no, that one's the longest . . . Look, I understand it already, you've been explaining it to me for an hour! I can't help it if it doesn't make me laugh . . .'

'But if you'd understood it, then it would make you laugh. So . . .'

'Hang on a minute, on the course they told us to read the play, not to laugh at it!'

'Exactly.'

'I'm fed up with this, you're taking advantage of me having a broken foot. Maybe the play'll be funny when we act it. But for now I'd rather we stopped. Otherwise I have a feeling that by the time we put it on I'm going to be sick to death of it.'

The doorbell rang, rescuing Olivia from my futile literature lesson. She nimbly whipped the book out of my hands, and her face, which had been sullen for a good half-hour, lit up.

'They're going to be really surprised,' she anticipated with satisfaction. 'They're not used to seeing me keep still.'

'What's happening? Are you moving flats?'

Jean-Patrick was studying the cluttered passage in amazement.

'No, I'm tidying up. And don't try and come through that way, kids, you'll trample on my books. You'll have to go through the living room.'

'Oh well, it's obviously been a great success,' grumbled Jean-Patrick. 'And there was I thinking that you had to work.'

Suzanne assessed the damage, nodding her head.

'I'll help if you like,' she offered.

They still had their backpacks and coats on when they caught sight of Olivia, stretched out on her invalid's sofa and smiling modestly. She opened her arms to them.

'*Hel-lo*, children!' she boomed, her eyes wide. 'So there I was on the stepladder when – bang! – I fell off and – crash! – I broke my foot. It's no joke, is it?'

Thomas was immediately worried.

'Does it hurt?' he inquired, looking warily at the bandaged foot.

Suzanne gave a dismissive shrug.

'You're supposed to be a clown and you hurt yourself falling over, that's not very clever, is it? What are we going to do about school? Are we going to have stay in the homework room every day and wait for Mum to pick us up?'

'No,' Olivia replied, 'I'll sort it out with Marion's mother. You can come home with her. I'll be waiting for you here, on the sofa.'

'I can't leave you two on your own for five minutes,' said Suzanne.

I pretended to scold her. 'Don't speak to us in that tone of voice, if you don't mind, you impertinent little miss. We're grown-ups, we can do what we like with our weekends.'

She grumbled and I took her in my arms and twirled her round the room. 'Impertinent, impertinent,' I sang into her neck. She smiled, trying not to look too pleased. 'Hey! Look out for my hair! Can't you see you're messing it up?'

As I stacked slices of courgette in a glass dish, I made a swift calculation. Since I had been old enough to help in the kitchen, making and serving up food, I could pride myself on having prepared almost ten thousand meals, often with simple utensils and limited ingredients. I had cooked for intimate groups and vast gatherings. I had cooked by myself, or in tandem with others, with Cécile, or Agnès, or Jean-Patrick. I had derived varying degrees of satisfaction from it, sometimes profound and pleasurable, occasionally poignant. Sometimes I couldn't have given a damn and I'd let a fish in bread-crumbs go black in the bottom of the frying pan as I drank Muscadet. But if I was only allowed one room in the house, I'd vote for the kitchen. We'd all be sleeping at the foot of the fridge.

It was time to sit up at the table for dinner. I didn't want to move Olivia in case she put weight on her foot, which I thought might be risky the first evening after a sprain. She, meanwhile, wasn't keen on being supported to the family table. We would have been forced into close proximity. I would have had to hold her by the waist, she would have had to put her arm round my shoulders, it was more than likely that our skin would have touched. She'd rather have starved to death.

'I'll carry you,' Thomas said obligingly, but he was too small.

Finally we decided to take our plates over to the sofa. I put tea towels on the floor and we improvised a picnic which made us all happy, particularly the children. We all love a change of scene.

Once the children were asleep, I felt like going to bed as well. My head was ringing; swarms of wasps were buzzing back and forth between my ears and stinging me en route – quick, luminous stabs of pain, which dazzled me.

'Do you need anything?' I asked Olivia.

'No. Do you?'

'No, nothing except sleep.'

Her face grew serious and full of concern.

'You shouldn't make yourself so unhappy. You shouldn't feel like leaving us. It's too much,' she said.

'Don't worry,' I replied, 'there's no chance of me doing anything, since you've nicked all my pills. Quite apart from the fact that now I've got to tidy up all the books and look after your foot.'

'All the same,' Olivia mused, 'I can understand me behaving like a jerk. But a woman like you, who's got children and work and a family and an education, for a woman who's got all that to want to do away with herself, that I just can't understand.'

5

In all probability, Olivia saved my life that year. I'm not just talking about that appalling weekend, but also about those other months of my existence which she filled with her constancy and grace.

She took up residence on the sofa, from where she watched the television and made phone calls all day long. In the evening the children helped her, a pair of meticulous little valets, enchanted by being able to wait on her. Marion's mother dropped in occasionally on the way back from school for news of the foot. She settled down at the side of the invalid with the copy of *Les Précieuses Ridicules* and followed long passages with her finger as Olivia glumly reeled them off.

Mme Alvez brought us awful doughnuts dripping with oil which she'd tenderly cooked for Olivia. We exchanged a few words on the doormat, but she refused to come in, even to say hello to the recipient of her gift who was hailing her excitedly from the end of the sofa. I wasn't sure what she dreaded the most, our untidiness or ungodliness. So I gave up trying to persuade her, and accepted the greasy paper bag, thanking her in a whisper, with all the fussy ritual of a geisha. I was afraid that my rowdy voice and my sudden movements would harm her. Stiff people seem very fragile to me; they can't bend, so if they break, they break in two and then it's the end of the world.

Thomas ate all the doughnuts — he liked Portuguese doughnuts. He also liked Japanese seaweed, golden couscous and crimson borscht. What he didn't like was French cooking. He thought it was depressing.

'A French family eating French food, don't you think that's a bit National Front?' he asked innocently, chewing on a rubbery doughnut.

'Don't talk with your mouth full,' answered Olivia, who didn't give a damn about politics.

The living room had begun to look like a military camp, as everyone brought in their kit and unpacked it on the spot according to some random logic. Pyjamas, toothbrushes, biscuits, books and schoolbags were scattered everywhere. My files and computer had taken up permanent residence on the trestle table. At supper time we moved them out of the way and I admonished the kids for carelessly strewing Coco Pops over the keyboard.

Then that weekend finished, Monday came and I had no choice but to get back down to work, to return to manufacturing the meaningless hype which generated nothing more worthwhile than money at the end of the production line.

I don't know whether it was the vodka, from which I hadn't really sobered up, or whether it was the Lysanxia, with which I was still saturated, but I typed all week in a state of hilarity. The facts hadn't changed: the work was the same mixture of contemptible benefits and contemptible exploitation as before. But it no longer provoked the impotent rage of which so often I was the helpless victim. I was no longer so desperate for the world to turn over a new leaf. I was indifferent to both the losers and the winners. I didn't care about anything.

This comfortable cynicism lasted until I read an article about the living conditions of children in Peru. And until a PR shared with my answerphone her rage and confusion on having received an appallingly written report, an offence to both her eyes and her budget. What had got into me all of a sudden, had I gone completely mad?

These events reminded me of two truths. The first: however much I wanted to consign both victims and executioners to history, without siding with either, this unworthy world only thought of itself in the present, and in the present, things were neatly sawn in two. I had to resign myself to deciding where my allegiances lay. The second: just because a job is idiotic, that doesn't mean that it's any less work. The shameless collaborator in this unworthy world must work just as hard as the person of integrity who denigrates it. Often they have to do even more. I could try not to care about anything as much as I liked, but it wasn't going to get me out of my predicament.

'Well, for a start, if you didn't spend half your life on that scooter, you wouldn't have so much trouble with your back.'

Denis was lying on his front. I was sitting astride him and massaging his back authoritatively.

'Stop wriggling, I can't feel what I'm doing any more.'

'Let me see,' Denis said and turned over, sending me flying. 'Why don't you become a masseuse?'

'Oh, very funny.'

'Don't laugh. You'd be excellent at it. You'd have lots of clients, no boss, you'd be paid cash and at least you'd be doing something useful.'

'But I'm not trained – I don't know anything about it.'

'So what? Do some courses.'

'I haven't got time.'

'Make time. In three months you'll have changed profession.'

'I don't think so. And turn over, we haven't finished.'

It was one thirty. I had made some tea and Denis was peering at me short-sightedly. I thought he looked peaky; he wasn't getting enough sleep, hanging around in bars, clubs and snooker halls, out every night like a young raver, although in his defence it had to be said that he *was* young. For a week he'd had a revolver in the box on the back of his scooter; a guy had given him it in Pigalle one night, and then disappeared. This revolver was making him very worried. He didn't know what to do with it. Should he throw it in the Seine? He couldn't decide and it was driving him mad.

He had also decided to get me out of my rut.

'I've got it. Plumber. Find out, there must be training courses. You'll have a whole female clientele. They're always being ripped off by con-men in overalls, they'd be bound to prefer you: I would anyway. Wow, that'd be so sexy if you were a plumber.'

I agreed delightedly. I've always loved the idea of wearing overalls and rubber boots. Of playing a part in the normal course of things. Of doing work whose effect on the world could be measured.

'Plumber, not bad.'

'Florist. Gardener. Cook. Picture framer.'

Denis was stopping me getting to sleep.

6

When Olivia knew *Les Précieuses Ridicules* off by heart, she stood up from the sofa and felt the ground with a crumpled foot. Then she risked it. She launched off and crossed the living room in one go. We all had a little trouble finding our places now they no longer radiated round the sofa.

As well as learning Molière, Olivia had also rung around and found work. She was going to be an activities organizer at a holiday village: one of her friends, who was thick with the owner's daughter, had pulled some strings. The village was offering her a trial week somewhere; she wouldn't know where until the last minute, it depended on requirements.

'They're very interested in my clowning courses,' she told me. 'I'll put on shows and I'll look after children. As long as I'm with kids, it should be alright, what do you think?'

I didn't think much. But since I'd never been on a package holiday, I couldn't really dissuade her.

'You can always see how it goes,' I suggested, restraining myself. 'A week isn't the end of the world.'

In a way I encouraged her. I wasn't indifferent about her working. I was looking forward to her being able to provide herself with a decent income, and a secure future. I myself, though, didn't want to work at all.

Whatever I was doing, I lost interest. I ran out of ways to keep my eyes open during meetings. I'd sit down in an armchair, my notebook in my hand, and pinch the thin skin of my wrists until I drew blood; I'd bite my lips; I'd smile winningly like a waxwork at the Musée Grevin. But it was no good: my pencil still slid drowsily to the bottom of my piece of paper.

I bought a Dictaphone, but I kept forgetting to listen to it and losing the thread. I'd sit frozen and mute opposite some disconcerted businessman for what seemed like hours while he waited for my questions and looked at me as though I was mad.

I only had to sit down in front of my computer to feel my intellect disintegrate. I searched desperately for words which didn't seem to come any more. All the sentences I'd thought were forever etched on my memory, ready for reuse, had vanished. I paced about. My mind rambled. I thought about the Kalahari desert. The chimpanzees in Vincennes zoo. My children. A Haydn concerto. I thought about how lovely it is to go swimming in a cold pool and allow your mind to be filled by a stream of repetitive images.

I'd spend five hours on a task that should only have taken twenty minutes. I handed in my commissions late. I made excuses – a child at death's door – so as not to have to hand in anything at all. I had kidney trouble, appendicitis, shingles, a breakdown, a bereavement, so sorry, all the best.

I stopped answering the phone. Every day my answering machine recorded a litany of threats and menacing encouragement. I didn't listen to it, I wiped the tape; we were quits.

I had always been lazy. Cowardly, too: fear of the consequences had always been enough to keep me on the straight and narrow. But suddenly I didn't care any more about what might happen tomorrow. Today was enough to worry about.

I came back to the flat early in the evening. I peeled and julienned some vegetables, browned them over a low heat in a casserole and then covered them with water. I kept an unnecessary eye on the pot as I read the paper. In a word, I made soup.

I had lunch with Laurent, with Agnès, with Cécile. I went to the cinema in the middle of the day, laughed at the funny films and shed copious tears at the others. I was full of enthusiasm. I didn't want to die at all any more.

The rumour went round that I was making a mess of my work. Mylène got fed up with it, then Jérôme and the others, which was only fair enough. I had fewer and fewer commissions and I became used to the idea that soon I wouldn't have any at all. My bank account was drying up. After I'd spent the money I had earned in the last few months, there wouldn't be much to look forward to. I'd have to live off thin air.

'Why don't you take a sickie?' suggested Agnès.

She obstinately refused to understand that I wasn't entitled to sick leave, or days off, or holidays; I belonged to no one. As such, Social Security, which was only too happy to take my money when I was earning, was not prepared to give me any back when I wasn't.

'And I'm not going on the dole, Agnès, before you start,' I said to her, 'you know what you can do with the dole.'

'I can lend you twenty thousand francs,' Laurent offered. 'You don't have to pay me back.'

'Thanks,' I said, 'that's a lot for you and not enough for me.'

'Well, in that case, you can come and live with me when you're thrown out on the street.'

'In a two-bedroom flat?'

'We'll squash in.'

I squeezed his hands for a long time under the table and he settled the bill.

'I can lend you two thousand francs,' said Denis, having considered it for a while, and I kissed him emotionally. I knew very well that he didn't have two thousand francs; he'd have to borrow it himself before he could lend it to me.

'Lord,' I thought at night, 'I've tried to be in two places at once for years. I've done enough now.'

Drowsiness would settle on my eyelids and I'd fall asleep. I dreamt of God: his insouciant ways, his lilies-of-the-field and his birds-of-the-air; I dreamt of Martha slaving away and Mary lolling about. I liked praying. The world is a more comical place with God than without.

7

'No,' said Thierry.

I had just opened the door and found him standing on the doormat.

'I've come to tell you that it's no. I got the results this morning. The test came back negative.'

'Phew,' I said.

'Here, this is for you, it's a present.'

He handed me the package he was carrying under his arm.

'Wow, it's heavy.'

It was a mirror in a gilt frame.

'A mirror,' I murmured, 'that's a good idea.'

'I found it an antique shop. It took them an hour to wrap it up.'

I admired the mirror, turning it in every direction and feeling its weight; but there was nothing special to discover. He must have paid a small fortune for it: a mirror, what a mad idea.

'I'll help you hang it,' he promised.

I leant the mirror against the sofa and we lay flat on our stomachs and studied our reflections. I agreed that it was a good mirror, handsome, and yes, we could see ourselves very clearly in it.

'I think I've found a job,' said Thierry after the mirror had been put somewhere safe ready for future hanging. 'For a company that makes fancy dress. I'll be designing costumes and masks and getting them made up. It's a good idea, don't you think? They asked me to write an application letter. I know what I want to say, that's not a problem, but I can't write. I'm going to come across as an idiot.'

'Do you want a hand?'

I picked up a notebook and my pen and sat down attentively.

'Let's go.'

I asked a question. Instantly the circuits in my idle brain sprang into life. I covered pages with my neat writing. Now it had woken up, the old wiring was still in good working order.

I typed the letter up while Thierry made coffee. Then he sat at my computer and changed nearly all of it.

'You're not offended, are you?' he asked.

'No, I'd rather you went over it. A piece of writing has to belong to someone's voice, otherwise it's meaningless, and what's the use of that?'

I could talk. A few days earlier I had been unforgivably tactless.

'Does the name Annie Fratellini mean anything to you?' Olivia had asked me. She suspected I didn't know that many people.

'Yes, she's very famous.'

'I want to ask her about a summer course. I rang her up and her assistant told me that I had to write a letter. Can you help me with it?'

'What do you want to say to Annie Fratellini?' I began.

'That I want to do a course. I just told you.'

'Yes, but why?'

'Because I'd really like to do a course with her.'

'I've worked that much out, I'm asking why you want to do a course.'

'For loads of reasons. I don't know. That's why I'm asking you to help. I've never learnt how to explain myself. If I could, I wouldn't be asking you.'

'OK, but sit down here while I write it, I'd rather you stayed beside me, you haven't done that for ages.'

Effortlessly, I evoked my broken childhood, the laughter which had always got me out of trouble and allowed me to save face, the words lying dormant beneath my silent gestures, my desire to learn. I imbued the letter with fervour and restraint. I made it so that you could hear my heart beating behind my words. Then I signed it 'Olivia'. I tore the page out and handed it to her. I felt pretty proud of myself.

She took it without thanking me and read it. She stood up looking grave and went out of the kitchen with it. She didn't say a word. I guess she didn't have any left to say. I had taken them all away and stuffed them haphazardly into a fraudulent letter. It wasn't until she'd gone back up to her room that I realized, too late, that I was worse than stupid, I was wicked. Fratellini's answer came within the week, it was yes, soon. Olivia and I never spoke about the letter again.

But I thought about it. I remembered the Little Mermaid who swapped her voice for a pair of legs. She thought that you had to conform to be liked. She exchanged something good for something uncertain; her soul for the shell that encases it. Naturally, without a voice, she didn't get far. Three days later there was nothing left of her but a fleck of foam on the crest of the waves. We're never told what became of her voice. I don't think the witch who bought it ever used it for her own benefit. She must have forgotten it in a corner and done nothing with it. Silence. That was something for someone who stole voices to think about.

Thierry, thank God, wasn't the sort of person who allowed himself to be pressured into anything. So we spent a pleasant evening talking shop. We didn't discuss the results of the test or make any comments about it – what could we have said?

In the night he cried a few bitter, unconsolable tears.

'Why other people?' Thierry wept, his face buried in the pillow, 'Why not me?'

I hoped he'd fall asleep soon. I could have reminded him that we were all going to die, he and I included, time was tearing down the mountain. But I kept quiet. Just because something's true doesn't mean it's timely.

8

The holidays came. Olivia did an acting course, then she went to work at the holiday village. She returned tanned, ravishing, deeply depressed and plagued by a variety of illnesses. Thomas and Suzanne went walking with Jean-Patrick and their backpacks in the Pyrenees. Laurent triumphantly left his two-bedroom flat for a three-bedroom flat; he was either in love or preparing for our move. Denis chucked the revolver into the Seine in the middle of the night. Thierry signed up for a three month trial period at his new job, and Agnès asked for a raise which she got. Cécile fell out with Agnès, almost accidentally.

As for me, I slept and prepared my downfall.

'Hi,' Étienne Varlat said. 'I didn't wake you up, did I?'

'No,' I said.

He'd got me out of bed. I was holding the phone completely naked. I hunched up and hoped the people in the flat opposite were doing something a long way away from their windows.

'How are you?'

'Fine. I'm only in Paris for a while and I've just had to turn down a very stupid and very well-paid job. I wondered if you wanted it.'

'Oh,' I said, in a cracked voice, 'I couldn't take it on, thanks, I'm not working very much at the moment, maybe you heard.'

'Yes, that's pretty much what Patrick told me.'

'What does Patrick know about it?'

'Everyone knows, people talk. I thought you might need some work.'

'No, I need money.'

Étienne hesitated for a moment.

'I'm having supper with Guillaume this evening. You should come.'

*

Guillaume looked well. He had lots of colour in his cheeks, not because of the wine but because he'd been cultivating the healthy look since he'd left Paris for Montpelier.

Most of the restaurant's other customers had gone home. Étienne had just ordered a third bottle. The ashtray was overflowing and Guillaume was scribbling sums on the tablecloth.

'Listen to me for five minutes, will you,' he said, 'you keep on interrupting. Your rent would go down by a third.'

'Yes, but even so,' I equivocated, 'I'd still have to pay for flights to Paris . . .'

'I come here less and less. Once a month is enough. I use the fax or e-mail instead.'

'What about meetings?'

'They're done by phone. Or else you plan ahead and have them all together. Or you can only take work that doesn't need you to travel, like reports and books. But you know all this, we've been working for the same company for ten years. No one gives a damn where I live.'

'My set-up's even more straightforward,' said Étienne. 'Auxerre is only two hours from Paris. I live rent-free in my grandfather's old shack thanks to my mother, and I pay the rural rates which are nothing. I swear, as far as our work goes, there's very little difference between living in Paris and the suburbs of Rodez. Some clients even prefer freelances to be elsewhere. They like to imagine us in homespun robes, tinkering about on an ashram.'

'You should get away,' Guillaume continued. 'Your kids would love it. We could help you find jobs to start you off, couldn't we, Étienne?'

'But don't you think I'd find it difficult if I moved? I mean, I chose to live here, you know, I love it here . . .'

'But you'll always come back, even when you don't feel like it any more. You'll see; we think we love Paris but it's not true, we don't love it that much – not at any cost.'

'And what's stopping you from coming back in two or three years, when you've found your feet again?' asked Étienne.

One after another, the waiters had thrown in the towel. We were the only people left in the restaurant – us and the owner dozing behind his till.

'Let's go and have a drink,' Guillaume said, putting on his jacket. 'You two have got me all stirred up with your talk.'

'Is this a joke? You're not serious, are you?'

'Oh,' I said, on the verge of tears, 'of course I am, of course I'm serious.'

'But I've told you hundreds of times that you can come and live with me!'

'There's three of us, it would never work, we'd all go mad.'

'What, you don't think you'll go mad at Mum and Dad's? You're telling me you're going to move back into your old bedroom, send your kids to your old school, have supper every evening with the family and stay *sane*?'

'I haven't got a choice, Laurent. I know Mum and Dad won't throw me out; anyway, the house is big enough for all of us and I'll pay my way. I won't be far, you know. It's only an hour on the train.'

'An hour and half, actually. What do the kids think about it?'

'They agree with me.'

'And Jean-Patrick?'

'We've arranged to share weekends and holidays. I'll get a season ticket.'

'Oh shut up, please, I feel like slapping you.'

*

Denis approved unreservedly.

'Great, my mother's promised to give me her old Renault Five. I can drive down to see you; you can introduce me to your parents.'

'Whooah, not so fast.'

'OK then, I'll come at night. You can creep downstairs and let me in. You'll be very pretty, all rested and happy. We can take the children for walks . . . I could take photos. If you want a hand moving, give me a ring. When are you off?'

'Totally absurd,' was Cécile's opinion. 'Just the thought of living with my mother makes me want to jump out of the window.'

'I haven't got any other option.'

'So you say. You've got to *think*.'

'Yes,' said Olivia, 'yes, of course I understand.'

'Do you want to come with us? It's a big house and you liked my parents, I thought.'

'No thanks, I've got my courses – I can't get time off that easily. Don't worry, you know I always manage. I'll get a room in a hostel.'

'In a hostel?'

'A friend of mine's been living in the Salvation Army hostel on the corner of rue Faidherbe for a year. She says it's fine. I can get a place there – maybe a little two-bed.'

'But what about money?'

'That'll be OK. I can go back to the holiday village and I've still got my dole.'

'But you hated that job, it made you ill.'

'Yes, but I don't have to do it all year. Just enough to save up for my courses.'

She drank her coffee in little sips.

'I can tell you're worrying yourself sick,' she said kindly, 'you mustn't stress yourself out so much the whole time. This year's been really good, I've never stayed in one place for such a long time before. And we'll stay in touch. I've become attached to the children, after all — I'll want my visiting rights.'

Finally I told Thierry. He listened to me in silence.

'Laurent's right,' he said, when I'd finished, 'it's a stupid idea.'

'You don't know anything about it. My parents aren't the same as your parents.'

'So? It's still a stupid idea.'

'That's easy to say if you're single and you've never had to look after anyone other than yourself. If I was on my own, I'd be a smart-arse, too.'

'Have you asked your parents?'

'Not yet. I wanted to tell you all, first.'

'Do you think they'll agree?'

'Yes, people don't let each other down where I come from.'

'Hang on, there's something I don't understand about this. Are you going because you really want to live with your parents or are you going because you don't know what else to do?'

'Guess. I've given notice on the flat. We move out at the end of June. When I've paid for the move, I won't have any money left. My name's mud with all my old employers. And I've run out of steam. I'm tired and I need someone to help me.'

'OK,' said Thierry, 'Now I understand. Since you're moving, do you want to come and live with me?'

9

Olivia's sitting opposite me at Thierry's kitchen table.

Since she got here, I've made three lots of coffee with the espresso maker which I only bring out for her; normally I use the percolator Laurent gave me at Christmas. I'm pretending to read the paper and sneaking looks at her over the top of it, which doesn't seem to perturb her. Now she's thirty her face has grown more angular, accentuating her delicate cheekbones.

Before I started writing we had a brief talk. She said, 'You can write what you want about me, I don't mind at all. But you've got to be careful, I don't want to hurt anybody else. I'd rather you lied. Alright, get a pencil, you can make some notes.'

Later I became worried. We talked about it again one evening when she'd dropped round for coffee.

'I brought you a little birthday present,' she said as she came in.

'That's sweet of you. I didn't do anything this year, not even dinner, I couldn't be bothered.'

'Oh, well,' said Olivia. 'Go on, open it.'

She watched me curiously as I unwrapped the little cube.

'Do you like it?'

'Yes, it's good to have one for night-time and actually, I'd just run out.'

'I'm glad you like it. I was a bit worried you wouldn't. I gave Armelle the same thing last week and she wasn't very happy. Apparently you shouldn't give people anti-wrinkle cream as a present.'

'Why's that?' I said blandly.

'Olivia,' I warned her, 'it's only my perspective, and perspective distorts things. You'll see. You've got to bear in mind that fiction's a complete jumble, some things in it are recognizable and lots is completely made up . . . and they're not people, exactly, they're characters . . . and it's not so much true as sincere, although I'm not so sure it is that sincere, come to think of it . . . and I'm not really talking about *reality*, or anything resembling it. Sorry, I'm floundering about; basically, what I'm trying to say is: it's not you. For instance, I don't know anywhere near everything that was going on with you back then . . .'

She made a noble and distant gesture with her hand, as though she was dispensing a blessing.

'Don't get worked up,' she declared, solemnly, 'it's obvious you're doing all you can, you just don't know it all.'

Her eyes left mine, her beautiful liar's eyes.

I insist that she takes a look at at least parts of what I've written, parts I think she might not agree with.

So she reads it while I wait. Sometimes she taps on the page with her finger.

'Yes, that's true,' she agrees.

'Oh, you remember that?'

'There's something you've left out.'

She looks up at me. She's enjoying herself.

'Oh, God, *that* one, if only you knew . . .'

I wave my arms vigorously.

'Help! Stop!' I say, nearly shouting. 'Don't tell me, I don't want to know anything else. If you start again I'll never get to the end of it.'

She gives me a mocking look.

'Don't panic,' she says, 'what's past is past.'

She carries on reading. Then she looks at her watch.

'I'm not going to have time to read it all. I can't hang about, I'm meeting someone at one.'

I leave her to it for a while. I've got pins and needles in my legs. I go out of the kitchen and sort out the washing in the ironing basket.

She calls me back in. She is rubbing her hands and laughing her little-girl laugh.

'I'm going to send this book to my brother-in-law. That'll show the bastard.'

'No way. You want to give my book to someone I'd like to see dead?'

'OK, OK – but I really would like to, it would teach him a lesson.'

'Nothing's going to teach him a lesson except maybe a good stretch in prison. If you want to teach him a lesson, all you've got to do is report him to the police.'

She sighs and says nothing.

It's nearly midday. Olivia gets up from her chair.

'I've got to go now.'

'Five more minutes. At least read the passages that might be embarrassing for you.'

She puts on her jacket.

'Forget it, we've already talked about it. How's Thierry, is he well?'

I lock the door of the flat. She goes down the stairs ahead of me.

'Which way are you heading?'

'To the station. I'm meeting Suzanne and Thomas there from school. They're going to spend the afternoon with Jean-Patrick and I'll see them onto the overground train.'

'Aren't they old enough to take it on their own yet?'

'Yes, it's just me, I guess, I prefer to put them on, just to check they've got their tickets and they're on the right train. You never know.'

While I'm justifying myself, Olivia looks at her watch. Suddenly, she's found some spare time.

'I'm coming with you. I can get the Metro from there. I haven't seen them for two months.'

We hang around under the local departures board. I buy us some *pains au chocolat*; they're warm and greasy and the pastry sticks to our fingers.

Olivia chats.

'Guess what happened to me?'

She's been working for some friends of Dr Cajoudiara and now, all of a sudden, he's going to be passing through Paris. He left a message on her answering machine, saying he'd like to meet for coffee.

She says casually, 'I've been meaning to ask you. When you live with a man, is it normal for him to want you to stay at home? I need to travel, I need to work. Does that mean that I don't really love him? Maybe I don't need to love anyone, actually, you know what I'm like, I can't do it. What do you think? Oh, this chocolate really sticks to your fingers, you haven't got a tissue, have you?'

She fills me in.

'Sometimes I feel shattered. I've really got to start taking Prozac again, maybe I should have some proper analysis, sometimes I think I haven't changed after all, that I'm just the same, and then the depression comes back and . . .'

'But it's not you that's changing, thank goodness, it's your world, look at it: your diplomas, your boyfriend, your flat, your friends, your job, the play you're rehearsing. Here you go, here's a Kleenex.'

The years have passed and she's still as talkative as ever.

I study the minutes as they tick away on the board. At last I catch sight of Thomas and Suzanne, pale and luminous in the reflected mother-of-pearl light as they come in under the glass roof. They spot us and start running from the end of the concourse, their heavy bags throwing them off balance. I step back as they reach us. They're taller than Olivia. She seems small in their arms.

*

The train pulls away. We wait behind the ticket barrier until it has left the station.

'Have you got time for a drink?'

'No,' says Olivia, 'I've got to go and see a women's rights representative. I met her at a conference and she wants to have a talk. Rehearsals don't start until June and I've got a bit of time so I arranged to meet her.'

'When's your play?'

'November. Will you come?'

We are at the top of the stairs, our faces buried in my Metro map.

'I'd go by Montparnasse if I was you,' says Olivia.

'But I always change at Châtelet, and then at Concorde.'

'Gosh, don't you know how to read a map? Look, it's not very complicated, you just have to follow the orange line with your finger, there you go. Anyway, don't worry about it, we're taking the same line. You can come with me. What are you doing at Pernety?'

'I'm meeting Cécile, we're going to see a film.'

She gets out at République. I stay in the almost empty carriage. I pull open a seat and sit down. The automatic doors close. I watch her through the window as she walks away. Her bag swings at her side. She doesn't look round, she's in a hurry, she's got things to do.